the
girl
who knew
there was
more

the
girl
who knew
there was
more

SHELBEY KENDALL

To my three special gifts,

Bryson. Remy. Adlee.

It is a mother's wish of a happy life for her children that most desire, but I have been bold enough to hope for more. I hope for a life that is rooted in knowing the One who intricately designed you. I hope you live your life fully even when it isn't happy. I hope you silence the lies of the world and rest in the truth of God. I hope you use your life and your gifts for something more.

With all the motherly love I have to give,

Momma

INTRO

Her feet fit in regular, plain boots. Her body fit into a regular, stifling dress. Her mustard locks were dull. Her green eyes, pale. Her brain worked normally—nothing special about how it operated. She could do math equations, punctuate correctly, and remember the market list in her head when her mother sent her on Saturday mornings. But that heart.

Her heart felt everything. Every emotion overcame her frail body. There were days she wasn't sure her chest could keep it locked in place. The beat of it felt magnificent. It beat with a triumphant confidence and a doubtless knowledge that she was meant for something else—that there was something more for her.

But her brain fought her, constantly informing her that she wasn't special.

How could someone so ordinary ever become someone extraordinary?

1

It was just an ordinary day, like most days. She rose from her ordinary bed and put on her ordinary clothes. As she was smoothing out the dullness of her gray dress, she noticed a slight tear in the bodice and her heart beat with the thrill of an opportunity to buy something more colorful, more vibrant, and maybe something with some sparkle.

But her head began its daily reminders…

You aren't special.

No one notices you.

What makes you think you deserve a dress that would make you stand out?

You are ordinary.

Her heart wanted to speak up but it wasn't as bold as her head. She'd silenced it many times choosing reason over hope.

"Breakfast, Ava!"

She hated the name her mother called her, but she said it was best Ava had a simple name. Her actual name, Avisha, sounded too splendid in a world that was simple. Her mother didn't want others to make fun of Ava or exclude her because of having any other name but an ordinary one.

"Coming!" Ava shouted back with a slight irritation in her voice.

She shimmied on the ugly, gray dress as her brain told her that she was being unreasonably moody. She tried willing her brain to understand the dilemma. She wanted her brain to understand the pain that ached within her heart, but it didn't listen. It never did.

She gave a quick look into her hazy, old mirror that had a long crack right down the middle. It was an antique, her mother had once told her, and she was fortunate enough to have a mirror that reflected at all. Her faint, green eyes stared back at her from the reflection. Ava saw the sorrow that made her look more tired than she was. She desperately wished she loved what she saw.

"Something is wrong with me, dear friend in the mirror. I don't feel like I belong in this boring life. Maybe if I lived somewhere else or looked like someone else, I would be happier. My heart longs for more, but I'm just an ordinary girl destined for ordinary things."

She started to look away from the mirror but caught half of her reflection not moving along with the rest of her. Her eyes widened as she grabbed the edges of her rough, wooden dresser staring deeper into the mirror, willing something amazing with all the strength she could muster.

"Dear friend in the mirror, do you exist outside of me?!" The words tumbled out and hope filled Ava's breath. She could feel her heart quicken its pace.

And then her brain had to make itself known.

Silly girl, a mirror is just a mirror. It would be utterly ridiculous to believe your own reflection had a life of its own.

Ava sighed, agreeing with her brain, but she could feel her heart did not.

After a bland breakfast, she took the lunch her mother had packed in a plain, brown sack and headed down the street to school. As she strolled, she took in the muted tones of all the buildings, wrapping her morning walk in a frame of bleakness. Sometimes, she felt like the color had been drained away in this place and it made her feel melancholy.

Melancholy was one of her favorite words. She believed it defined the essence of her life. She looked it up a couple of years ago in the worn school dictionary after first discovering the marvelous word in a novel she had been reading.

Melancholy *(noun)* a feeling of pensive sadness, typically with no obvious cause.

When she had first read the word, it had sounded incredibly depressive. However, the word also made her sorrow feel a little more magical. When she defined her life through melancholy, Ava could allow herself to be consumed by a gloomy spirit—snuggling into her decided sadness. There was an air of mystery in her suffering, and she believed where there was mystery, there was wonder. It was a wonder that confirmed the feeling in her heart that there was something more.

Her steps came to a halt in front of the faded, brick schoolhouse. Placed on top was an overwhelming reminder of the sadness that echoed through the streets of Dryden. It was an old, rusted bell that no longer worked. Ava had never heard it give a clanging melody and it made her wonder when it had given its last ring of joy.

Dryden was the town where Ava lived. It was a bleak spot on a map, but the only place Ava had ever known. In fact, no one Ava knew had ever traveled outside of Dryden. It was as if Dryden was all that existed, and the thought depressed Ava even further. The town was full of people that expected everyone to live in misery. In fact, the school in front of Ava was the same school that had continually shaped the citizens of Dryden into the dullness that the town was known for. Ava hadn't heard laughter in the classroom since she had dared let a giggle slip out during her first year.

When she had come home that day after feeling the judgmental stares of her teacher and all her peers, she had asked her mother why the people of Dryden seemed to be like gloomy, storm clouds. Her mother had responded with a shrug that turned into a gentle hug. No words were given, as if her mother didn't even know why everyone seemed to cling to disappointment. What could have happened for the place where Ava lived to become so colorless?

It only added to the mystery she felt in her own melancholy.

"Hi, Ava."

A voice jolted her from her swirling thoughts.

It was Jack. Jack was Ava's best friend. They had met at lunch a few days after she had giggled in the classroom. He had approached her while she was sitting alone on a dead log under the shade of an enormous tree. He had smiled and Ava had felt the comfort he offered her.

Jack had plain, brown hair that matched his plain, brown eyes. He wore clothes colored a drab gray that matched hers, and his shoes were always scuffed since they were handed down from his five brothers that wore them before him, but Jack had never felt ordinary to Ava. He always had a smile for her, even on the days that were hard for him.

"Hi, Jack." Ava didn't break her gaze from the rusted bell in the sky before them.

"What are you thinking?" Jack inquired.

"I'm trying not to let my brain speak. It's been cruel this morning," Ava replied.

"Maybe some math facts will whip it into shape." There was a bubble of humor in Jack's voice.

"At the very least, it will be subdued." She took a step towards the schoolhouse, not allowing her melancholy to melt even if Jack always tried to warm it. She entered the chilled building absent of posters or decorations, too frivolous for the place Dryden shaped their perfect citizens. A simple, large chalkboard hung at the front. Rows of simple, worn desks lined the rest of the dreary room.

Class droned on for what felt like centuries until their teacher, Mrs. Polly, finally dismissed them. Before allowing them to properly line up and leave the room, she delivered bland report cards on every desk. Ava stared down at hers, an ugly "B" mocking her. The truth was everyone received a "B". It made everyone feel average together. It was a badge of conformity.

Mrs. Polly cleared her throat and then said, "I know our winter break is long, but please keep up with your studies. I'd hate to make you repeat what you've learned over these short months."

Ava's heart began to pitter patter. She could feel it swell with hope, believing there was possibility for a day that wasn't ordinary during winter break. She was thrilled to be released from spending her days surrounded by the depressing room full of peers that were drained of color.

But her brain, even in its exhaustion from a day of math facts and cursive correction, piped up.

It's just winter break. Full of boredom. Full of chores. Full of nothing.

And Ava believed her brain was right. What kind of magic had she ever been able to discover on any break before now? What made this one special?

"What are you doing over winter break?" Jack's voice interrupted the depressing thoughts in her head.

"I don't have any plans," Ava sighed. "Two months is an awfully long time. I've never understood the length of winter break."

"It's been that way since *The Neverending Snow*." Jack's tone turned surprised. "Do you not know about *The Neverending Snow*?"

Jack often spoke of things that didn't fit in with life in Dryden. Ava often wondered if Jack's imagination created things that blurred fantasy with reality, making him believe things that were not factual.

"That sounds too magical for our world, Jack." Ava rolled her eyes, feeling the blandness of the day wearing on her face.

"Dryden wasn't always the way it is now." Jack's tone was serious.

"Jack, stop talking nonsense." Ava's voice was firmer than she intended it to be. She saw the hurt infect Jack's disposition like a deadly poison. Her heart also felt the venom of her disbelief in her rejection of a possible unknown history.

"It's not nonsense, Ava. If you'd quit acting so sad all the time, maybe you'd open your eyes to what could be." Jack's response was filled with agitation and Ava felt bad about causing it. Jack was the only friend she had. She wanted to believe him; in fact, she believed deep down she did. However, reason had worn her over the years and it defined what she thought was real and what had to be fiction.

"I have to go," she said sullenly.

She started to walk away so she could be left alone in her melancholy, but Jack's voice followed her.

"You know, your world would change if you would simply smile."

Ava's heart felt the stab of Jack's words. Her heart was always wanting Ava to smile and embrace possibility. Her heart longed for her to explore the feeling that there was something more.

Ava kept walking. She didn't want to respond to the truth in Jack's words.

Her brain rationalized with her, forcing her submission to its reasoning. She knew it was on a mission to defy any hope that was attempting to survive within her, and yet she listened.

You don't need Jack. He speaks of impossible things that will only feed your heart with ideas that will create trouble for you. There is safety in doing what you are told and becoming who they want you to be.

A tear slid down her lackluster cheek. She knew it was safer to do what was expected, but her heart broke at the thought. How would she ever know if there was something more if she didn't dare to believe in it and search for it?

Ava kicked a rock on the dusty, dirt road as she walked home. Jack had told her that the streets of Dryden had once been paved and smooth. They had even glittered in the sunlight as if tiny diamonds were embedded in the concrete. If it was true, they must have been torn out before Ava's memory began. She couldn't remember a day when there wasn't dirt beneath her worn, black boots that were now covered with a brown film from her footsteps that had become a shuffle. Her disagreement with Jack had drained her of all energy and her heart throbbed in anguish from their argument.

She challenged her brain once more, trying to imagine a world different from the Dryden she was surrounded by, but she couldn't picture it. The day had depleted her of any hope she had.

Maybe one day she'd be brave enough to believe her heart as much as she believed her brain, but today was not that day. She also knew her brain was right when it came to safety. She couldn't afford to lose anything else. She'd already lost her father.

2

Three weeks had passed. Winter break was proving to be a lengthy disappointment that seemed more exhausting than attending school five days out of the week. Time seemed to stretch on forever. Ava's brain took the opportunity to snatch onto every gloomy minute and fill her head with the continued narrative of melancholy. At least in the classroom her brain had been kept busy by mundane tasks.

"Ava, you must get up and do something." Her mother's voice felt distant as Ava's attention was directed at staring out the window into the gray skies while lying on the couch. Her hair tangled around her heavy head. She hadn't brushed it in days, and it had become a nest of knots even a bird would abandon. She ran her tongue over her teeth that were coated with the residual of all the tasteless meals she'd helped her mother cook. She also knew she smelled like desolate dreams and rancid sweat. It was a smell that would even repel the rodents that sometimes broke into their home hoping to discover a spare crumb to fill their tiny tummies.

She laid unmoving which prompted her mother to say more.

"Ava, what am I going to do with you? I can't just let you lay there looking as if you are sinking into the deepest pits of despair." Her mother's voice was brimming with concern.

Ava finally looked up at her mother, willing herself to focus on what her mother was saying instead of burying herself into the gloom she'd created over the last three weeks. Her mother's face confirmed that Ava looked like death reincarnated.

"I'm fine," Ava managed to mumble.

"You are not fine, Ava. You haven't left the house in weeks." Her mother's hands were placed on her hips and frown lines drew themselves on her forehead.

"What's the point?" Ava muttered the question as she rolled away from her mother.

Suddenly, she heard her mother stomp her foot.

"That's it, Ava. It's time you had a bath and put yourself back together. I thought you'd be able to shake yourself out of it, but it seems I am going to have to do the shaking myself." Her mother's voice turned forceful which made Ava grow with irritation.

"I'm in mourning, mother."

"Of what exactly?"

"My life." Ava rolled back over to face her mother. She had accepted the fact that her life couldn't be what her heart longed for—a life that wanted something more. Her brain had convinced her that giving up her dreams was best, but her heart had shattered, and Ava was grieving all she had once hoped for.

Her mother glared down at her, and Ava realized her mother wasn't just frustrated; her mother was angry. She hadn't meant to make her mother angry, but she also couldn't understand how her mother was completely fine living such a sorrowful life every single day in a place that felt so hopeless. Wasn't her mother bored? Didn't her mother want more? Couldn't she see how miserable life was around them?

"Your life?" her mother exhaled the question. Then her anger turned to something else that appeared to be guilt tugging at her face. "This is my fault. I'm going to fix this."

Ava immediately sat up, her eyes growing wide. "Fix what?"

Her mother didn't answer, instead she stomped off, determination ringing from her footsteps. Ava heard clambering in the kitchen as her mother threw pots around, filling them up with water to boil so Ava could wash off her stink from the last three weeks.

Ava slowly lifted herself from their torn, scratchy couch. Her brain and heart were both in shock trying to determine what her mother meant by fixing something. Her mother had also never yelled at her, and she hadn't seen such guilt on her mother's face since her father had passed.

Her mother was considered ordinary when it came to women in Dryden. She dutifully performed all her tasks and always looked put together in her drab shades of gray. Her brown hair was always pulled back in a tight bun and a piece of cloth that matched her dingy dress wrapped around her head. Ava began to wonder if she'd ever seen her mother's hair down. Was it a plain, mousy brown or was it a vibrant, shiny one?

Ava stood up, feeling the creaky floorboards beneath her bare feet. When she was younger, she'd believed the old floorboards were magical. The squeaks and groans voiced the memories of forgotten families who lived there before them. However, that was when she was ignorant, and she now knew they were just old floors in need of a good sanding and polish or replaced completely.

"Bath is ready, Ava." Her mother's softness was back, but a glint of something else subtly sparked in her eyes. "Please wash up and brush your unruly hair. I must run an errand. I'll be back soon."

Ava's mother wiped her hands on her apron before untying her strings to hang it up.

"Mother," Ava's voice was weak as she said, "I'm sorry. I didn't mean to upset you.

Her mother didn't reply. She simply gave Ava a small smile and then pointed to the bath before she left their house.

Ava had to admit the warm water felt delightful, as if it were melting all the worries that had turned her into the moping monster she'd become the last few weeks. Her heart fluttered, waking up from the neglect Ava had given it. She took a deep breath and plunged under the surface of the water.

Her hair danced beneath in buoyancy. She could feel it exploring, desiring to discover any new thing that may be hiding beneath the bubbles. Ava kept her eyes closed, not allowing reality to seep into her brain to ruin the moment. For a second, she felt something within her that reminded her of how she used to feel. A version of herself that believed in magic even when the world and her brain hushed her hopeful ramblings.

Ava's breath couldn't hold much longer, but she wanted it to last forever. She quickly opened her eyes, inspired by a gurgle of hope in her heart. The bubbles from beneath bounced the light from the window, making them appear iridescent.

Ordinary things made extraordinary! her heart exclaimed.

Her brain rushed to take the discovery and replace it with something less optimistic.

But then they pop. Things that seem good always end, her brain added.

Ava broke the water's surface, replenishing her lungs with ordinary oxygen, feeling the beat of her heart slowing down.

"Maybe some people get a chance to embrace extraordinary things," she whispered to herself as she wiped the bubbles from her face. She hoped she was one of those people, but she also felt doubt.

She had brushed her hair and it was almost dry when her mother rushed through the front door with a large, brown paper sack. Her mother's face seemed frazzled. Ava never saw her mother frazzled. She was usually the picture of perfect calm.

Ava watched her mother take a deep breath as she melted into the chipped, faded door behind her.

"My hair is finally brushed," Ava quietly declared, hoping to break what felt like a thick covering of worry over her mother.

"Next time, don't wait three weeks," her mother replied as she composed herself. Ava watched her place the brown sack on the kitchen table as she smoothed her dress and straightened her shoulders. She then smiled softly and turned to face Ava.

"As usual, no wrapping paper could be found in any store, so this brown paper sack will have to do," she began. "I know your birthday isn't for a few months, but you seemed in desperate need of this gift. I probably should have given it to you much sooner."

The velocity of Ava's beating heart pumping could have sent her to the moon and back in that moment. It propelled her forward to the package and her brain didn't have time to catch up. Presents were precious and rarely given in Dryden.

Ava looked at her mother and back at the paper sack in front of her, waiting to be given permission to rip into the sack, even though she knew she would not rip it. This sack could be reused.

"Go ahead," her mother nodded.

As she unfolded the flap concealing the contents, Ava saw color and her heart leaped.

She carefully removed a container filled with the rainbow. She'd never seen such vibrancy. She then removed a book filled with blank pages. Last, she removed beautiful, golden brushes wrapped in a single piece of lace.

It was so extravagant. It was so unusual. It was extraordinary.

Her mother's voice broke through Ava's wonderment, "There are some rules that apply to this gift. Items like this are not easily found in Dryden and if found, they usually disappear. First, you must keep this gift hidden when not in use. Second, you must never tell another soul you possess these items. This is a secret between you and me. The next rule is not really a rule, but a warning. Items of this nature can inspire much larger things to come to life. If this happens, you must listen to both your brain and your heart. They need to learn to guide together instead of resisting one another. The brain and heart are fickle things with their own agendas that can lead us astray."

"Mother, where did you...? How did you...?" Ava's voice trailed off. She'd never seen anything this beautiful at any of the stores in Dryden. Everything she had ever seen was practical and mundane.

"No questions, Ava. There is no need for you to know," her mother chided.

For the first time in a long time, Ava smiled. At first it was small, but it crept across until her entire face lit up with such immense excitement that she was sure her face would split in two. Was it possible to smile that big? She wasn't sure, but she felt as if her mouth had reached her ears.

"This is the most fantastic thing I have ever seen." Suddenly her lips felt wet. She licked them tasting salt and then discovered she was pouring tears.

"Oh Ava, there is no need to fuss so much over it." Her mother may have been trying to respond sensibly in that moment, but Ava noticed the upturn of the right side of her mouth. "I must get supper together. I will dismiss you from your supper chores so you can find a suitable hiding place for your gift."

Ava gathered the supplies up in her arms and she felt like she was holding the world or the world as it could be and not just what it was. As she made her way up the noisy stairs, she felt her brain trying to create an argument of reason from its initial shock of the recent development.

Finally, her brain said, *What is the purpose of painting if no one will be allowed to see it?*

But to her relief she heard the voice of her heart, *Not all things are meant to be praised by others. Some things are meant for more.*

A thrill danced up her spine as she closed her bedroom door.

"Brain, you will have to learn that you don't know it all."

And with that, she began the search for the perfect hiding place.

3

The night felt forever long. Ava's mother had told her she had to wait until morning to use her new painting supplies. Her mother had said daytime held the best lighting for painting, but how would her mother know? She'd never painted. However, Ava realized she didn't really know much about what her mother might know. Ava was curious how her mother even knew how to locate the painting supplies.

She also knew her mother had always taught Ava to comply with the duty, quiet, and order that was expected in Dryden. Dryden expected manners, routine, and minimal fun. The absence of fun was preferred. It's why laughter, smiling, and any activity that had to do with color or creativity felt forbidden. Ava hadn't ever seen a painting, a storybook, or piece of clothing that had any color or character to it. Everything Dryden encouraged attempted to keep its citizens in a bland sameness.

But Ava also remembered the words Jack had told her on the last day of school before winter break, *"Dryden wasn't always the way it is now."*

So, what was it like before, and why did it change?

Ava was impatiently waiting for the sunlight to stream into her curtainless window. She rarely closed her shutters. She loved when the bright beams gently poured inside her room, staining her white walls, and worn floors with a golden hue. She'd always enjoyed how the sunlight danced with the dust particles in the air. It may not have been actual glitter, but she had sometimes imagined her room was being showered in fairy dust that could transport her away to magical lands.

I'm not sure painting is a great idea with the windows so wide open. Her brain was rested and alert for the day, already at work planting doubts.

It seemed as she grew older, her brain grew in doubts. She'd always noticed how the adults in Dryden were more somber, but the misery of the adults eventually became the misery of the children. It was utterly annoying, and now that Ava really thought about it, it was sad, too.

However, this morning, her heart was more confident than it had been in years, and it beat with a mighty reassurance.

What if what you've been wishing for comes from those paints and brushes? her heart murmured between its thumping.

That's all Ava needed to adventure forward, and why would her mother give her something if she wasn't meant to use it?

The sun finally made its glorious appearance. The beams greeted the dirt in the air turning her room into a glittered paradise. Ava felt a bubble of hope within her. She stumbled quickly out of her bed, rushing to the broken floorboard underneath. It wasn't a large hiding space, but it was perfect for the gifts that her mother had given her.

Her hands tingled as she pulled each item out, handling them with precious care. Her heart hummed; she had never felt it so alive, as if something spectacular was upon her.

She scooped up all her supplies and ran the few steps to her desk.

But you don't even know how to paint, her brain stated, continuing with its practiced disbelief.

Her brain's doubt was valid. Ava didn't know how to paint. She'd heard of a paintbrush, of colors, and of art but she had no lessons or experience. She'd never even seen a painting before, so how would she know what to do?

She shrugged her shoulders, choosing the hope of her heart.

"It can't be that hard," she mumbled. She quickly grabbed her cup of water she kept beside her bed during the night. Water. Paint. Paper. Brushes. She took a deep breath, nervous to ruin a piece of precious paper but tingling with excitement of the possibility.

She dipped the paintbrush gently into the cup of water, watching the bristles dance as they loosened their grip of one another. She glanced over at her colors, suddenly panicked about what to choose first, but the deep green called out to her. She'd never seen such a rich green.

A refreshing rush blew through her as she slowly moved the brush along the top of the green in her vibrant palette, a whisper in her soul breathed life and she imagined billowing, soft grass waking up tenderly to a warm breeze. She could feel how it gently brushed against her calves and when she looked down at her paper, the grass she had imagined was perfectly painted.

She gasped.

Her mind reeled, but her heart soared.

I told you some things are meant for more! her heart exclaimed. She could feel her heart thumping, the beat matching her breath.

Ava's nerves held her frozen, however she couldn't help but feel amazement at the beauty in front of her. She'd never seen grass so alive. It contrasted greatly to her surroundings, as her bedroom was empty of any color at all.

She rinsed her brush in the cup of water, mesmerized by the swirling shades rippling within it. Then she concentrated on her palette of colors, hope pulsing through her that she'd feel a pull to the next color. The blue burst in front of her like a shower of sparks. Her heart burst along with it. She pulled her brush into the calmness of the color envisioning a sky she'd never seen. She imagined a sky that held beautiful, blending blues. She felt clouds moving above, shifting into shapes that made her mind dizzy. When she looked down at her paper, a vibrant sky filled with fluffy clouds stared back at her.

This doesn't make sense, her brain finally spoke up, waking from its shock.

Sometimes things don't need to make sense, we just have to believe. Her heart felt sure, unlike her brain. It was all she needed to pursue the next color, and the next, and then the next until the page in front of her was erupting with hues and life she'd never seen before with her own eyes.

It was a field of green grass, with wildflowers of pinks, purples, and yellows tangling with the blades of grass in a delicate dance. The sky was open above, making room for opportunity in a way that freed your lungs. Surrounding the field were groves of trees in deep greens, encasing the field in comfort. In the distance, a deer stood majestically, demanding respect from its stance.

Ava couldn't believe it. She'd just created the most wondrous thing she'd ever seen, and it didn't make sense how. Her knowledge and skills in painting were nonexistent. She only possessed her own desire that fueled her with a quiet hope she'd be able to create something delightful, something that would make her believe there was something more.

She closed her eyes and timidly fluttered her eyelids back open; afraid the painting would vanish in front of her. That's when she saw it. The grass in the painting moved. Her eyes widened.

That's impossible, her brain said.

Or is it? her heart responded.

Ava stared long and hard at her painting. Minutes passed; the painting unmoving.

I told you, her brain said with arrogance in its tone. Ava's shoulders slumped as she stood up from her desk. Her body ached from sitting. She wasn't sure how much time had passed, but the sun had cleared her bedroom window.

She made her way to her cracked mirror and stared at her reflection intently, "I think I'm going crazy, mirror friend."

Ava studied herself, washed of color. It felt cruel that a painting could contain such vibrancy but life itself felt drained of it. The crack through the middle of her mirror divided her imperfectly, more of her nose residing on the left side than the right, and more of her mouth residing on the right side than the left.

"I want to believe," she said quietly. The words were barely audible. Ava wasn't even sure if the words had truly left her lips at all.

Then part of her face, the part that existed to the right of the crack, changed. It was slight but her hair glistened golden instead of falling flat over her shoulders. The green in her eye deepened as if the paintbrush she'd used to paint the trees had painted her eye as well. Her cheek even had a rosy flush to it. It was a soft pink that made her skin glow, where her other cheek was an ashen gray that made her seem hollow.

Was she crazy or was there something more that she'd never noticed before?

Go back to your painting, her heart prompted, but she was glued to the right side of her mirror. Her plainness had fallen away giving a glimpse into beauty she'd never seen in herself. She'd imagined herself more colorful and confident but imagining it and seeing it were two completely different things.

Doubt crept in. All the thoughts her brain had ever told her about being plain and ordinary soon filled her head.

"That's not me. That can't be me."

As she said the words, the color drained from the vibrant half of her reflection to match the faded half. Sadness overcame her as she allowed herself to feel inadequate. Soon, she allowed anger and panic to take over and she charged at her desk full of colors. Ava glared at the painting, now sure that something was wrong with her. She wasn't supposed to create beautiful things. She wasn't meant to be different from everyone else. What she had just done was dangerous. Painting was forbidden.

Fear struck her, and she frantically began to clean up and hide what she had just done. If anyone stole a glance at what she had created, they'd surely punish her for it. She stuffed the supplies in the broken floorboard and scowled at the painting. She felt a hint of pain as she wadded it up and stuffed it deep into the hiding place.

She grabbed the darkened cup of water, carefully ran down the stairs to empty its contents into the bathroom sink, and watched the water full of wasted color disappear.

Her heart cried but her brain seemed smug as it said, *Smart girl. It's not worth standing out, Ava. It's dangerous. Who knows what would be said about you.*

And she knew her brain was right. The people in Dryden would disapprove and come to steal any color she had left in her life, draining her to shades of gray.

4

Ava scrubbed the dishes harshly, her fingers turning red from the rough abrasion. Her face wore a scowl and her body felt tense with aggravation.

"This is not how I expected your mood today, Ava," her mother said. Then, she lowered her voice and added, "Was the painting difficult?"

Ava met her mother's eyes that matched hers, wishing her mother could read her thoughts so she didn't have to speak. She felt ashamed in what she wanted to tell her mother. The gift was beautiful, and the painting had been one of the easiest things she'd ever done. She didn't know what potential trouble her mother put herself in to give her such an extraordinary and rare gift. She didn't want to seem ungrateful, so she lied.

"I just didn't expect it to be so hard," Ava muttered.

"Some things just take time, Ava. It's like baking. The first time I attempted to make those buttery rolls you love so much was a disaster. I wasted much flour and precious butter growing my skills for them to become what they are today. You can't expect everything in life to be easy." Her mother pulled her into a tight hug. "You'll get it. Just give it time."

But Ava didn't need the time as her skill already seemed mastered. She felt guilt as her mother held her and her bitterness grew for the paints that hid in secret under her bed. She was drawn to them, but she was also fearful of them. She knew if she continued to paint, she would continue to believe there was something more, and that something more could end up being very dangerous. She'd surely end up doing or saying something that would make people talk.

Her mother had helped mold her life to be one that allowed her to fit in. She couldn't set herself apart. She had to accept that she couldn't become someone special. The paints made her feel like she could be special, so she took that moment wrapped in her mother's arms to silently vow to herself to never pull them back out. She wasn't worthy of them. She was destined to become what everyone else expected her to become.

"I think I'm going to go see what Jack is up to." Ava pulled away from her mother, attempting a feeble smile.

"That's a wonderful idea. You haven't seen him this entire break. It's about time you had a conversation with someone other than your mother. I'll finish the dishes." Her mother tied her drab apron around her waist while waving Ava away. "Off you go!"

Ava reluctantly shoved her weary arms through the starch sleeves of her black wool coat. Her arms were too short to make their way to the end. It was one of her mother's old coats. Ava grew too quickly, and a new coat was a waste if you could make it without. She tried bunching the sleeves up, but the sleeves continued to tumble back down. Frustration boiled up in her chest and she let out a garbled cry.

"Let me help you." Ava's mother stepped in front of her gently and began to carefully roll each sleeve to a proper length that would allow Ava to pull her scratchy, gray gloves on. Her mother finished both sleeves and then took the gray hat she'd knitted for Ava the year before and tugged it over Ava's head.

"Thank you," Ava mumbled, slightly embarrassed by her temper tantrum that was better suited for a toddler.

Her mother placed a kiss upon her forehead, and she grabbed both of her gloved hands. "Emotions are not a bad thing, Ava, but it is best if you learn to control them instead of allowing them to control you." She then let her hands go and opened the door to the bitter world outside. "Be home for supper."

Ava trudged through the filthy snow. Five days into break, the snow had begun its descent from the skies to the earth. It covered everything, but when everything was covered in dust, dirt, or soot its pristine white was instantly soiled. The snow in Dryden was never pretty, even the icicles that hung from the peaks of the sad little shops and houses along the streets were smudged in brown. She'd heard the term 'winter wonderland' before but Dryden just felt like a winter wasteland.

Her boots stuck in the sloppy mud underneath the covering of snow as she made her way to Jack's house. Jack lived in a small house tucked behind the woodshop where his family worked. Jack's father never smiled, but everyone knew he was pleased he had six boys to put to work and carry on the family business. A small curl of smoke unfurled from the beaten chimney missing several bricks. She could smell a stew brewing with spices her own mother never bought from the store. Jack's mother practically lived in the kitchen feeding her seven men. There was always a feast at Jack's house.

She didn't have time to knock before the door swung open. She was greeted by one of Jack's older brothers, Tommy. His permanent scowl rested on his face.

"Ava," and then he turned and yelled, "Jack!"

"Thank you," Ava said meekly. She never liked any of Jack's brothers. The older they grew, the more unpleasant they became.

Jack's sunny disposition should have been clouded years ago in this household.

She saw Jack scrambling towards the door, tossing a drab scarf around his neck as he stumbled into his scuffed pair of boots. Jack's smile contrasted greatly from the face of the brother that still stood unmoved by the door.

"Hey, Ava! I'm coming! Hope you are up for a walk." She knew that meant he was thankful for a chance to escape. She didn't blame him. She felt a pang of guilt realizing she should have come several days ago, but she didn't know how he would receive her after their argument. She should have known Jack would always be happy to see her.

Jack's mother yelled, "Home by dinner!" as Jack slammed the door releasing icicles all around them. Jack laughed at the shattering of ice at their feet.

"I don't think I need to ask how your break is going by the intensity of your departure," Ava said as Jack pulled his arm through her own. "But whatever your mother was cooking smelled divine."

"Mom prepares the best meals, but you wouldn't know it with the lack of gratitude shown from my brothers. I always make sure to give her extra compliments, so she never thinks her hard work goes unnoticed," Jack said. "I would invite you back, but the food probably isn't worth the company of my brothers."

"I have to be back for supper anyways," Ava replied. "Even though I'm sure the company wouldn't be as bad as you say." She tried to make Jack feel better about his brothers even though she was secretly thankful her mother wanted her home.

Jack stopped and looked her over.

"Is there a problem?" Ava murmured with a confused look on her face.

"I haven't seen you in forever. I just wanted to make sure you were okay," Jack stated.

"I know I should have come sooner. I may have fallen deeper into my case of melancholy. This is the first time I've left the house since class was dismissed." Ava realized how good it felt to stretch out her legs even if her dull surroundings affirmed her dreary spirit.

"You really need to stop embracing so much melancholy. It doesn't suit you well. You'd be better if you fell into a state of jubilation! I feel that jubilation would look good on you." Jack gave her a hopeful smile.

"What is there to celebrate?" Ava pressed.

"Life."

Ava gave a sarcastic laugh before she said, "I told my mother that I was mourning my life."

Ava then buried herself deeper into her oversized coat, suddenly embarrassed by revealing the truth in her own words.

"Well, that's a silly thing to say when you have so much life left to live. Why mourn something when you still have it?" Jack abruptly unlinked his arm from Ava. "I'll race you to the big hill!"

He didn't give her a chance to complain about how hard it would be to run in her boots through the snow and mud. He was off strides ahead of her. Snow flew all around him as his ungraceful movements plowed through. Ava wanted to laugh, and then her brain piped up.

That boy is going to get you in trouble.

She waited, hoping her heart would speak up.

"Ava!" Jack shouted. "Scared of a little fun?" His laughter bounced between the boring houses, making joy ring through the streets. She thought she saw a curtain move in someone's window and her nerves began to tingle. If someone caught them, they'd be the talk of the town.

You need to go home, her brain chided.

Ava didn't want to go home. She was growing weary from the thoughts her brain gave her. Before she allowed any more time for her brain to continue its narrative of anxiousness, she began running frantically forward. Her limbs felt like cream pudding, unaccustomed to the blood pumping through her body to carry her forward quickly.

"I'm coming!" Ava gasped. Her lungs felt punctured from the crisp air as she took it in.

She finally caught up to Jack. Clouds erupted from his lips as he laughed heartily. His cheeks seemed flushed, and his nose had even developed some color. She hoped she looked the same. They'd made it to the big hill and they both fell into the thick snow, all smiles and frozen tears as the cold pricked at their eyes.

"I was worried you were going to let your brain keep you from living again." Jack looked over at her with honest concern.

He wasn't the only one that had been worried. In that moment, Ava felt her heart flutter a soft thank you; and hope once again was restored.

When she returned home, Ava's entire body felt like an icicle.

"Ava! You are going to catch your death! What on earth were you doing?!" Her mother scrambled to her side, quickly removing all her clothes soaked in soggy snow.

"Jack and I played a few games. It's nothing the warmth of the fire can't fix," she replied brightly. She was still elated by the rush of throwing her best snowball and hitting her target of Jack's face. He'd instantly fallen in a pile of laughter.

Her mother stilled.

"We were careful, mother. We went all the way out to the big hill." Ava tried to ease her mother's worried face. Playing wasn't for-bidden in Dryden, but it was considered inappropriate behavior that should be corrected instead of encouraged. Laughter wasn't something the citizens of Dryden were known for.

"I just want the best for you, that's all." Her mother gave her a weak smile. "Go warm up. I just put a new log on the stove. It should be burning well."

Ava warmed up and ate her mother's cooking of dry turkey and unseasoned, mashed potatoes, but the excitement of her time with Jack made her imagine the meal was filled with flavor. She ate every bite with enjoyment until her plate was scraped clean.

"That was wonderful," Ava said. She remembered how Jack told her that he always made sure to give his own mother extra compliments to make sure she knew how appreciated she really was. "I'm off to bed! I'll be down to help you with breakfast in the morning."

She gave her mother a quick hug and skipped up the stairs. She was a completely different person from the girl she had been hours before. Ava arrived at her bedroom and began to dress for bed when suddenly she was frozen once more. However, it wasn't because of the cold. There, on her desk, laid the painting she'd made. She carefully took a few steps towards it.

It was smooth and crisp, no wrinkle to be found from her earlier crumpling.

Just believe, Ava. Her heart finally spoke up, more confident from the frolic in the snow.

Ava wanted to believe so badly. She wanted to believe something special and magical was happening to her. So, she stared into the painting with a tiny flicker of hope in her heart.

Quietly she whispered, "Please, please, mean something."

She saw the grass she'd painted begin to sway, the clouds begin to shapeshift, and the deer looked directly at her and blinked. Ava took a deep breath, closed her eyes, and when she opened them, she couldn't believe where she was.

5

The world Ava found herself in had a glow to it, as if magic touched all its edges. The grass tickled her legs while the soft fragrance of the wildflowers drifted up to her nose. Warmth seeped through her skin and when she looked down, her nightgown had been replaced with a cheerful, yellow dress with dainty lace peeking out from the hem. It was a color she'd seen in her palette of paints, but never in Dryden—a yellow she imagined reflected sunshine and smiles.

She stared into the distance; the groves of deep green even more vibrant than they'd been painted. The deer looked at her, unmoving. It was graceful and its antlers were grand. She imagined him to be the king of the forest, highly respected like a mayor of a town.

Ava was mesmerized but was scared to move. She wasn't sure if the magic of this place would disappear if she decided to investigate it further. She timidly took a step forward in the tall, wispy grass and nothing happened. Relief poured over Ava.

"Where am I?" she whispered the question in awe.

Suddenly, a man appeared. He was tall and his complexion glowed with the rest of the surroundings. His eyes were as brown as the trunks of the trees in the grove. He wore simple clothes of a clean, white shirt and tan trousers, but somehow, they didn't seem simple on him. He was barefoot which prompted Ava to look down at her own feet, realizing she was barefoot as well.

"Hello, Avisha." His voice was smooth, like a gentle, running stream.

She stammered, "How do you know who I am?" Goosebumps covered her skin like a second set of clothes.

He smiled the warmest smile she'd ever seen and said, "I've known you always." The way he looked at her made her believe she was special and that what he said was true. She felt as if he knew her in a way she didn't even know herself.

"And it's Ava," she said with slight hesitation to correct the man.

"That may be what the world calls you, but what do you prefer?" The man looked at her with what felt like overflowing kindness and his eyes sparkled with a genuine softness. She looked at him for a while, debating her name. She'd always wanted to be called Avisha.

"You can call me, Avisha," she finally said.

"Avisha, would you like to take a walk with me?" The man offered up his arm to her. Ava didn't hesitate to place her arm through his. There was something about this man that made her feel safe— not just a safety that he would protect her from danger, but a safety that exuded deep comfort. Ava felt like she could trust him to lead her where she needed to go.

They began making their way through the grassy field, their bare feet gently sinking into the soft earth, footprints lingering behind them.

Ava finally gained the courage to ask the man a question, "What is this place?"

"Where do you think we are?" he replied.

Ava dug through her thoughts, trying to find an answer. Minutes passed before she realized her heart held the answer and not her brain. She smiled slightly and then looked up at the man by her side, "I think this is the place where hope exists."

He smiled back at her, "Hope does exist here, Avisha, and it also exists in your heart. That's why your heart knows this place, but I also know you doubt your heart a lot." He paused his words along with their step and turned Ava to face him. "Sometimes we can't live life by what we only understand. Sometimes we have to believe there is more."

Ava's heart beat faster hearing the words she'd always wanted to be told.

"This place is beautiful, majestic even," the man kept talking. "Glory grins here knowing this place is worthy of it. You'll find magic in the simplest of things, this place glowing with something your heart has believed in."

Ava broke her stare with the man to gaze over all that surrounded them. It did appear worthy, even though the place was simple. It was a vast field of wild grasses and flowers, not a building built from gold and diamonds, but it felt as if the value here was equal, maybe even more than any worldly riches she'd imagined. Compared to Dryden, it was unlike anything she had ever seen.

"Do I get to stay here?" Ava asked, already beginning to dread her life outside the painting.

"One day," he said, and it sounded like a promise.

"Can I come back soon?" She was hopeful, but also willing to beg if needed.

"Open your heart and embrace what makes you special. Do not fear what you've been given but give gratitude to it and you'll find yourself in places you've never been before," he said and then he was gone and so was the colorful scenery. She was back in her bedroom, staring down at the painting. The painting was still beautiful, but it paled in comparison to where she had just been.

She hadn't been gone long; she could still hear her mother's whistling downstairs.

Whistling?! Her brain sounded surprised, and she was surprised alongside it.

Had her mother always whistled? Ava couldn't recall. Maybe she did when she was younger or maybe the magic had followed her back from the journey into the painting? She wasn't sure if that was possible, but what seemed possible an hour ago was much less than what she believed now.

Ava stepped towards her mirror and the girl that smiled back at her had a little more color in her cheeks and a little more shimmer to her golden hair than she'd had that morning. It made her smile a little bigger.

She grabbed the painting off her desk and carefully placed it under the loose floorboard. There was a new belief within her of how special the painting really was. She turned her glass lamp off and slipped beneath her cool covers. She knew she couldn't tell anyone what had just happened or where she had been. She didn't even know how she could try to explain that she had just traveled through her own painting. She wasn't even supposed to paint. People wouldn't laugh, they'd mock her until she was beaten back into complacency.

But Jack might understand…her heart carefully suggested.

But if he doesn't, it might all be taken from you. Her brain reminded her of the expectations and rules in which she lived.

She sighed into the darkness, disappointed in the place she called her home. It was a place where she feared judgment from others and made choices based on their approval, even when it was approval from those she felt sadness for. If Ava was honest, the people in Dryden lived lives that reflected everything she didn't want for herself.

She laid there in the stillness and a tear gently rolled down her cheek. She thought back to when they had lost her father. He had become terribly ill, a sickness that slowly took small pieces away from him at a time. At first it was his body and his ability to move. Every movement had become difficult to make and soon the best place for him was his bed.

Even in her father's condition, he always had a smile for Ava along with thrilling tales that took her imagination to new places outside his bedroom walls. He always made her feel like she could become anything. One day, Ava had declared she wanted to be a princess and somehow, he had fashioned a makeshift dress from his bedsheets and wrapped her in them.

In his booming voice, he had announced her arrival to their humble abode, "Hear ye, hear ye! All within the walls of Lambert! Princess Avisha has graced us with her most regal appearance. How special it is to be honored with the visit of such a lovely princess. Everyone, please give their respect to the royalty before us."

Her mother had been leaning in the doorway to the bedroom, dark circles under her eyes but a gentle smile upon her lips. She had stepped into the room and made a slow and extravagant curtsy in Ava's direction.

"Why princess, thank you for coming to visit your humble servants." There was a delicacy in her voice that Ava had found a thrill in as she watched her mother participate in her father's games.

Ava had given the best curtsy she knew how to give at the age of eight. At the time, it had seemed grand; but it had probably been a silly sight of deep concentration that had produced a wobbly bow. It was one of their last days of laughter together. Soon after, her father began to lose his voice.

With her father's voice wavering, the voice in Ava's head began to speak up more often.

The town of Dryden was unkind to her father. They didn't like the way he lived with his arms wide open to possibility. Her father expressed gratitude often and found joy in the smallest things. His schooling hadn't shaped him into what the people expected of him. Jack often reminded Ava of her father.

Ava thought they would take silent delight in his sickness, muttering quietly to one another that he deserved it. Maybe they had, but first they relished in the sadness that overcame Ava and her mother when her father finally gave his last breath.

The people of Dryden surrounded them in gloom and Ava hated to hear their words of sorrow. She didn't know how they could genuinely be sorry for the death of someone they harshly rejected. She also didn't understand why they acted as if they cared. It felt fake and her heart had hurt. She had told herself she couldn't end up like these people, unkind until tragedy struck. She didn't want to become someone that only cared when darkness fell over others, she wanted to care about others when sunshine warmed them, too.

But sunshine rarely fell on the people of Dryden. It seemed they preferred the cloak of dark.

6

The next day Jack was sitting on the scratchy, green couch in Ava's house. The memory of Ava's father was still playing through her head from the night before. She wondered how life would be different if he'd stayed healthy and well.

"Jack, do you remember my father?"

Jack smiled, "I loved your father."

Ava smiled back at his genuine reply.

"He was one of the most joyful men I've ever known, maybe the only joyful one. He always had the best stories. One time, I tried to repeat one to my own father and he hushed me up quickly. My father has no imagination, and he feared the repercussions of such silliness in my head."

"Is that the time you couldn't visit me for a week?" Ava laughed, but also felt a pang of sadness for Jack and the relationship he had with his father.

"Yes," Jack laughed. "It was worth it. Your father's stories were one of the only things that made me smile." Then Jack's face fell in a shade of grief.

"I miss him, too," Ava said softly while grabbing Jack's hand.

"He was a good man, Ava, no matter what others said." Jack looked at her with a fierce determination. "He was a light that was needed, even if others didn't understand."

Ava turned her head away and fixed her gaze on the cloudy window showcasing the streets of Dryden in its winter landscape. For some reason, today didn't seem as dreary as the day before. The snow didn't seem as dirty, even though a new blanket of it hadn't fallen.

"What do you see outside, Jack?" Curiosity of how Jack saw things pulled at Ava.

"A thick covering of glistening snow coating the world with something new. I wish it could come down forever, wrapping us all in the freshness from where it came," Jack marveled.

Ava marveled along with him and his beautiful description.

"Yesterday it looked more brown than white," she murmured, wondering if he noticed how the earth stained the snow.

"Well, I suppose you could focus on where it is dirty, or you could look at where it is clean," Jack mused. "What do you think your father would see?"

"Probably whatever you see," Ava said while giving Jack a faint smile.

Then she felt her brain considering, even though it had nothing to say; but her heart said, *I told you ordinary things could be made extraordinary.*

In that moment, Ava believed it. She looked through the window with Jack choosing to see the white of the snow instead of the brown of the dirt. Maybe she had simply been looking at things the wrong way for too long. Her father had been gone for too many years and her optimism had gone with him.

She debated dragging Jack up to her room and showing him the magical painting, wondering if more than one person could travel through it. She didn't want to be alone in her secret. She wanted confirmation that what she had discovered was real and not a dream, but something held her back.

Snow swirled through the door as her mother burst through it. Ava immediately stood up to greet her mother and take the bag she'd brought in with her. The bag was heavier than usual.

"There was a special on beef steak today and I know we seldom have it, but I felt we could do with a splurge this week." Her mother's voice held a little more enthusiasm in it than Ava was used to. First, the whistling and now a somewhat cheerfulness about preparing a meal they rarely had. Ava wondered if her mother had always been this way and she simply hadn't chosen to see it like the snow and the dirt, or if something was different about her mother.

"That sounds amazing, mother," Ava replied as she lugged the bag to the kitchen table.

"Oh! Hello, Jack! It's been so long since I've seen you. How are you? How is your mother?" Ava's mother knew all the polite questions to ask.

Jack stood up to hug Ava's mother and then answered her questions, "I am doing well, Mrs. Lambert. My mother is also well. Thank you for asking."

"Would you like to stay for supper? We will have plenty." Ava's mother extended the invitation and Ava hoped he would agree to it. His brightness had been much needed for Ava's heart and head.

"I actually must be leaving, Mrs. Lambert. Thank you so much for the invitation. Maybe next time." Jack smiled at Ava's mother and then turned to Ava. "I must get home to do my chores, Ava. I enjoyed our afternoon. Thank you for keeping me company."

Jack grabbed his worn coat and placed his wool hat on his head before tipping it in Ava's direction. Then he opened the door into the world turning dark and was gone before Ava managed to say her goodbye.

Supper was delicious, filled with flavors she hadn't experienced in a long while. Her mother had cooked the steaks perfectly and Ava had fixed a side of rice and carrots. Her mother had even let her use some salted butter and garlic, giving the sides a rich aroma and a savory warmth. They sat at the table with their stomachs wonderfully full.

"How was your afternoon with Jack?" Ava's mother inquired.

"It was good," Ava said, but the afternoon had also prompted her to ask her next question. "Mother, what was your favorite thing about father?"

A misty haze came over her mother's eyes. Her disposition changed to an overly soft one.

"He was my favorite person," she finally said.

"But what was your favorite thing?" Ava asked again.

"I have too many of them," her mother said wistfully.

"I'd love to hear them all." Ava's voice was quiet, hoping her mother would be willing to say anything and everything about her father.

Her mother sat silently for several minutes. Ava was nervous she'd dismiss the conversation. It had been a long time since they had talked about her father. The air felt heavy around them, breathing was becoming challenging. Her mother took a deep breath and so did Ava.

"I loved the way he would think I was asleep, but he still placed a kiss upon my forehead and tucked the blankets in around me tightly, cocooned overnight until I shed the blanket in the morning. I loved the way he laughed. It wasn't like most laughs. It was deep and hearty as if he allowed all his joy to surface. I loved the way he cared about others even when they didn't care about him. He was given so many opportunities to respond with unkindness, but he didn't. Most of all, I loved the way he loved you. His eyes would come alive at the sight of you, filled with hope in who you were but also in who you would become. So many times, we'd end the day smiling at one another knowing what we had created was such a gift." Tears were quietly streaming down her mother's cheeks. "I was the luckiest woman alive to know a man so wonderful and I hate that you don't have him anymore."

Ava sat, unmoving. Her mother said all the words she'd wanted to hear. They were filled with evident love, but also great sadness. They'd lost the man that existed as the magic that brought hope to their life in various ways. He didn't create magic through anything shiny or through being well liked by other people. It was through words, through actions, and through his ability to find joy in what mattered.

"Mother, why did people not like him?"

The question hung in the air between them. It was something she'd always wondered. She didn't understand how a man who was so wonderful could be so hated.

Her mother sighed, "Oh, Ava. The world is sometimes cruel even to people who are not." Her lips closed and her words stopped, but Ava could see the contemplation in her mother's eyes. Ava hoped that meant she would add more. To Ava's relief, she did.

"Your father was one who never cared about what other people thought. He had lived in Dryden all his life, just like I have. We went to the same school you go to, which is where I witnessed your father's stubborn ability to go against what was expected. He wasn't ornery or one to cause trouble. He just didn't agree with much of what the citizens of Dryden were expected to become. He wanted to play, to laugh, to enjoy, to find more in the ordinary. His father, your grand-father, was a street sweep. He kept everything clean and orderly. Your father wanted more. He asked why they couldn't paint upon the curbs or place ornate lamps along the walks. His questions weren't out of disobedience but out of curiosity and wonder. The people didn't like the ideas he had."

Ava imagined the streets of Dryden colorful and filled with light pouring from beautiful lanterns suspended in the air above them. Would the streets remain dirt or would they be smooth, dark pavement that ran beside the houses and shops like a creek of rich, maple syrup?

"Mother, have the streets always been made of dirt?"

She looked at Ava curiously, but a hint of anger flared on her face as she replied, "No."

Ava waited for more to the short answer. It never came so she found herself pressing for details. "When did it become dirt?"

Her mother looked away, tears forming–clouding her eyes. "When your father took over as the street sweep, he knew he couldn't make them magical, but he would dance in them. He'd smile and tap along the perfectly, paved roads allowing his joy to echo throughout the town. One early morning, before the sun woke up, your father skipped off to ensure the streets were prepared for the people of Dryden. When he stepped out our front door, he found the streets in pieces. Broken pavement littered the streets.

"Who would do such a thing?!" Ava exclaimed, fury filling her body.

"Your father never asked. Besides, he wouldn't have retaliated. It took him weeks to clean the streets filled with broken pieces of asphalt. He'd come home every day with his back aching and his hands red from picking up every single fragment and putting it in his wheelbarrow. He must have completed thousands of loads, but your father never complained. Instead, he smiled as he worked, and he whistled. He whistled a bright tune. I don't think the people of Dryden expected that from him." Then her mother laughed. It was a laugh that grew until she was crying.

"Why did he smile? I would have been furious." Ava was surprised by her mother's laughing. She couldn't imagine what she would do if something similar happened to her, but she was sure she wouldn't smile about it.

"As I recall, he told me, 'Being mad about what they want me to be mad about will only show my own darkness. I can choose to be light even when it is hard to be.'"

Her mother wiped her tear-stained face with her apron. Ava sat with a slight pout.

But they deserved to be hurt, too. Her brain spoke up for the first time that day, echoing how she was feeling about the situation. She was angry for her father and for how he'd been treated. She didn't understand how others could be so hateful when her father didn't do anything to deserve it.

"At the end of his life, your father didn't want to regret the things he had said or did, Ava. There were times I thought he should have stood up for himself more, and maybe he should have. I think it's okay to stand up for yourself. However, even if you voice how you were wronged, it isn't okay to live by how you were wronged. Your father never chose to be defined by what was done to him or said about him. Instead, he lived a way that reflected what he believed was good, even when it was hard."

Ava mulled over what her mother said. It was a lot for her brain to process. She could feel it working through the words. As her brain worked, her heart felt, and it finally said, *Maybe being hurt doesn't mean you are silenced. Maybe it just means you learn to turn your hurt into something else.*

She didn't know what that something else was yet. From her father's actions, he'd turned hurt into joy, but she wasn't sure how that was possible. There had to be something else she was missing to truly understand.

7

Ava sat at her desk—her paper, brush, colors, and water laid in front of her. It had been days since she'd looked at her supplies. She had been too stirred up with emotions to think about creating something. Her head and heart were confused by what her mother had told her. She hurt for her father and the struggles he must have gone through by others misunderstanding him, or simply choosing to hate him.

Just paint, her heart whispered. Even though her heart had felt hurt, it still hoped.

What good will painting do? This town has shown how they prefer people to live. Painting isn't part of that, her brain added.

Maybe it was a bit out of spite, but Ava wanted to be different from those who had been so horrible to her father. She let her emotions propel her to pick up the paintbrush and begin a brand-new piece.

At first, she began with gray, which then turned to blue, and then finally she was washing it all in a pristine white. She could feel an icy burst from the painting in front of her with every detail she added, fueled by her resentment of the world she lived in. Soon, she realized a winter landscape that felt more cozy than bitter had formed. Snowflakes in delicate detail softly fell over a fresh blanket of snow that appeared iridescent with the colors that peeked through. The sky above was a calm blue that felt opposite of her agitation.

Ava wasn't sure she wanted to go through this painting. It seemed too perfect and clean. She debated for a while, trying to decide if she should attempt to make the journey, but when she closed her eyes and took a deep breath, she felt a wintry bite nipping at her eyelashes. When she opened her eyes, she was in the painting.

"Hello, Avisha." The voice of the man from before was beside her. "You seem as if you are unsure you want to be here."

Ava looked around, taking in the winter wonderland. As beautiful as the painting was, this place had the same glow from before making it appear even more enchanted. The snowflakes fell gently and without rush—as if they were created with a peace that made them enjoy the fall to the earth. There was snow in every direction, no end in sight to its reach.

She took a deep breath and turned to the man to reply in honesty, "The painting appeared too flawless, and I was afraid I'd somehow dirty it like the dirt turns the snow to brown at home.

He smiled a deep smile, one that made Ava feel grateful she was honest, but also that made her feel as if her feelings were not the truth. "I can understand why you might feel that way, but that's not how the snow works here. It is not made dirty by what it covers, it instead makes what is dirty, clean."

Ava took a few moments to process what the man had just said.

"But how does the dirt not stain the clean white?" she questioned.

"This snow makes things new, cleansing all it touches," he replied with sureness in his voice.

Ava looked down, noticing the beautiful black boots on her feet. She was wearing a crimson, velvet coat with a soft fur that lined its collar cozying up to her cheeks. She stretched out her hands feeling the smoothness of the red gloves that felt like silk against her fingers, unlike her scratchy mittens at home. She couldn't see her head, but she could tell it was topped with something that felt just as comfortable. She was sure she stood out against the white snow, no place for her to hide if she wanted to.

"What is troubling you, Avisha?" the man asked.

Ava was beginning to believe this man was important. He'd shown up in both paintings, knew her real name, and had explanations for everything she'd asked so far. She didn't know who he was and yet, she felt she knew him. It was because of this that she frantically rambled her next words.

"I don't understand how people can be so hateful. How can they judge so harshly and go out of their way to hurt other people?" All Ava could think about was her dad discovering the broken streets and how his heart must have felt in that moment. She imagined his heart must have been as shattered as the streets were.

The man looked at Ava intently. "Where you live, Avisha, there will always be unkindness. The people there hurt and sometimes they don't know what else to do except to make other people hurt, too. It doesn't make it right and it doesn't make it fair."

Ava wasn't satisfied with the answer. It wasn't her father's fault that other people were hurting and yet, they had acted as if it was. They'd punished him for their own suffering. The man was correct in saying that it wasn't right or fair, but shouldn't they receive their own punishment for punishing her innocent father?

"You aren't happy with my answer," the man stated.

"It is wrong for people who are hurting to make other people suffer. My father was hated but was the kindest person I knew. Sometimes they wouldn't even acknowledge him in the streets. They did horrible things to try to hurt him, but he didn't ever try to return the pain. I don't know how he could do it. I would want them to suffer." Ava was slightly embarrassed to admit to what she last told him, but it was the truth. Her heart roared with anger out of cruelty shown to her father.

"Avisha, can I tell you a story?" the man inquired with a tender look upon his face.

Ava nodded her head.

"There once was a woman who sang the most beautiful songs. Her voice was soft and soothing. She wanted nothing more than to comfort everyone who was hurting in the world. She'd sing lullabies to crying babies, songs of reassurance to those who experienced loss, and songs of joy to those who needed a reminder of all that was good, but not everyone liked her even though she never did or said anything with ill intent. She simply wanted to use her gift of song to make the world a little brighter. One day, another woman who was jealous of her tender voice, brought her a gift. She brought a soup she had made herself. The woman with the sweet voice thanked her and proceeded to eat it, but the jealous woman had laced it with spices intended to harm. The woman's throat began to burn until it became sore and numb. The next day she tried to sing a lullaby and the song came out harsh and stifled. Days passed and she never recovered.

The jealous woman had destroyed her voice and with it, all the songs that comforted those who sought them."

Ava sat stunned. "Why would you tell me such an awful story?"

The man replied, "I am not finished. There is always more to the story if you can look beyond the hurt. The woman mourned her voice, but she still smiled at those who came seeking a song. She would explain that her voice had been lost, but her peace remained. She would then speak quiet, encouraging words over them while she held their hands in comfort. They would leave the woman's home feeling hopeful once more."

Ava's heart flared for justice, and she interrupted the story, "But that evil woman. She should have been punished. What an awful thing to do to a person. She stole the thing that brought good to others."

The man lifted his finger towards her causing Ava to press her lips back together in silence. He then continued the story. "One day the jealous woman came back. She had lost a baby. Her grief was heavy, and she had found no relief or remedy. When the door opened, she began to cry out of her suffering. The woman without song gathered her up in her arms and brought her inside. She held her while speaking soothing words over her, telling her about hope amid her sorrow. The woman left a new person, regretful for what she had done but with a peace inside her she had never had. You see,

Avisha, everyone hurts. It may be at the hands of someone else or it may be a loss, but there is a choice that comes with the hurting. We can embrace the hurt and then hurt others, or we can embrace the healing and then help others heal. The woman who lost her soothing songs chose healing and therefore, continued to help heal others."

"But her voice wasn't healed. It was still damaged," Ava argued.

"That isn't the healing I'm talking about, Avisha. She chose the healing of her heart so she could heal the hearts of others. Yes, her voice was gone but she could still comfort others. She still had the ability to help them find a peace beyond their understanding and beyond their own hurts."

Ava stood there for a long time, pondering what the man had just told her.

"I believe your father was one of those people," the man said gently to Ava, lifting her head to meet his eyes. "He could have chosen to hurt others, too, but he didn't. He kept extending kindness even when no one was kind to him. You'd be surprised how many people he helped find hope when hope seemed impossible, even if they did not say so."

Ava was quiet and then in a small voice said, "How do you heal a heart?"

The man gave her a huge smile. "Remember how I said the snow is different here?"

He bent down and grabbed a huge handful of it and sprinkled it over Ava. She laughed at the tingle of it, but the sensation was different. It wasn't cold. It was warm!

"This is the snow that makes all things new," the man said.

"But how?" The snow was warm, and it made things new? Once her brain would have mocked such ideas, but even her brain was beginning to wonder what was possible. After all, she was currently inside a painting she had created.

"It covers anyone who wants it, anyone who asks for it. It's for those who have realized life without hope is miserable. Life will be hard whether you choose hope or misery, but those who choose hope find a peace that overcomes and overflows." He grabbed Ava's hand. "Now, let's go play in it!"

They took off running together for a huge hill of soft snow that had suddenly appeared. They ran to the top of it and found majestic, silver sleds. Ava jumped down on one and felt the rush of warm snow covering her as she whizzed to the bottom of the hill, and she felt its comfort. She was laughing, and Ava realized she hadn't laughed so freely since her father was alive.

8

Ava woke the next morning with a smile on her face. Light poured in through her small, bedroom window and danced with the dust making her room feel magical instead of ordinary. It also reminded her of the warm snow that had dusted her last night. She'd gone up and down the hill many times, never tiring. She thought for sure she'd need to catch her breath, but it seemed the air in the painting was a different kind. It refreshed her instead of exhausting her. She felt more wonderful with every trek back up the hill.

None of this makes sense, her brain said rather quietly as if it were more curious than certain.

"What if it doesn't make sense because we don't ask the right questions?" Ava whispered aloud to her brain. She stretched out under her covers, feeling every muscle in her body tense, and then she relaxed them. There was only one week left of winter break, and she knew she needed to make the most of it.

She hopped out of her bed to the mirror across the room. Her reflection had changed. Even with the messy hair that needed tamed, her complexion looked rosier, and her eyes looked brighter. She couldn't look at herself and not see a difference in who she was before she began taking trips through the paintings. She was changing.

She went to her closet and picked one of her two dresses, but she didn't see its ugliness this morning even though it would be easy to compare it with the vibrant colors she wore in the paintings. She began to hum as she dressed and continued the tune as she brushed her hair. She'd decided she was going to tell Jack about what was happening, even if he wouldn't believe her.

She ran down the stairs with such an excitement that her steps sounded like thunder echoing through their small home. Her mother looked up from the kitchen stove with surprise. "What in the world has made you so spirited this morning?" she asked.

"Good morning, mother!" Ava stood up on her tiptoes and placed a kiss on her mother's cheek. "It smells amazing down here. What is for breakfast?"

Her mother looked inquisitive, but Ava watched her shrug the curiosity off as she answered, "The usual of toast and eggs." She turned back to the stove flipping over an egg in the pan.

"Sounds delightful. Is there anything I can do to help?" Ava asked enthusiastically.

"You are a completely different girl than the one that was so gloomy days ago. What is going on with you?" she asked.

Her mother placed the last egg on a plate and brought the simple breakfast to the table. She grabbed the butter and a jar of blueberry jelly they had made from fruit grown in their small garden over the summer.

"I just realized I can choose to be happy," Ava confidently declared. She eagerly dove into the breakfast her mother had made. She could feel her mother's eyes on her, watching cautiously. "I'm okay, mother. I'm more than okay. I'm fantastic!"

Ava's mother slowly sat down across from her and began buttering a piece of toast. Ava wasn't quite ready to tell her about the magic in the paintings. She wasn't sure how her mother would react, and she somewhat feared her mother might take it all away. She knew it sounded crazy and she wouldn't blame her mother if she became worried about Ava's mental health.

"What are your plans today?" her mother asked, still going through her movements slowly as she watched Ava.

Ava swallowed her breakfast and replied, "I'm going to go find Jack. I'm not sure what we'll do, but it would be nice to have company today while you are away at work." Her mother worked as a seamstress. Most of her work consisted of mending since the people in Dryden didn't buy many new things.

"I may be home late tonight. We received several pieces to work on yesterday before we closed shop," her mother said. "Do you think you can start supper? It will require a trip to the butcher for a half pound of whatever is on sale."

Ava smiled at her mother, excited for the excursion and kitchen to herself to prepare a meal. "Yes! I'd be happy to help."

"I'll leave some coins on the table before I leave for work." Her mother got up from the table and then added, "Don't stay out too long with Jack. You'll need to go to the butcher by four for the best choice of what he has on special."

Not long after her mother had left for work, Ava was pulling on her winter gear to venture out to find Jack. She opened the creaky, front door, and a burst of chilled wind numbed her face. She couldn't help but let a laugh escape her lips. Her neighbor was outside scooping her sidewalk and looked up startled. The woman sent Ava a scowl.

"Good morning, Mrs. Edmund. A beautiful winter we are having, isn't it?" Ava dared to reply with a cheery disposition and a smile.

Ava was positive she saw Mrs. Edmund's nostrils flare as she said, "It is very well not. The cold is dreadful, and the snow has made everything a muddy mess. You'd best change that tune of yours, young lady. You know such merriment is frowned upon."

Ava inspected Mrs. Edmund. Her sallow colored face was full of wrinkles created from frowns instead of laughter. In that moment she realized how sad she looked, even in her anger. Ava wondered what caused the sadness that had turned to bitterness on her face.

Instead of allowing the grumpiness of Mrs. Edmund to affect her, Ava gave her one more smile and said, "I hope you have a good day, Mrs. Edmund."

Then she skipped off to find Jack.

As she walked through the streets, she noticed many other people like Mrs. Edmund. Their skin was a hue of gray and their faces full of sorrow. They gave her unhappy glares if they heard her whistle or laugh, or if she greeted them with a bright 'hello'. Their lack of color and brightness contrasted against their surroundings which Ava noticed was more vibrant than usual. The color of the stores appeared a little shinier and the snow had a sparkle to it that set it apart from the dirt.

Maybe things aren't always what they seem, her brain pondered, echoing the feelings of her heart from days before.

It was in this realization that Ava remembered what her mother had said when giving her the paints and brushes. Her brain and heart needed to learn to work together instead of fighting against one another. Ava wasn't completely sure what was happening within her, but something about the paintings was changing her.

She found Jack behind his father's woodshop, stacking a new pile of wood that would be used to stoke the fire inside. She watched him for a while as he worked. His face didn't appear ashen like everyone else's had on her walk. He had a slight flush to his cheeks as he put every small log in its place. He also wasn't scowling. She wasn't sure she'd ever seen Jack scowl. He had always been annoyingly chipper on the days she had chosen to embrace her melancholy.

Jack suddenly looked up and jumped. Once he collected his breath he said, "How long have you been standing there?"

"Not long," Ava replied. "Are you able to take a break soon?"

Ava could feel her nerves tingling as the time to tell Jack about her paintings grew near. She knew she couldn't back out. She needed to tell someone about what was happening to her; it needed to be shared. She knew she needed to tell someone who would listen and possibly believe what she was saying. That's why she knew Jack was the perfect person to keep her secret safe, but Ava also thought he would believe, too.

"I'll go talk to my father. He's been scrambling trying to find things to keep me busy all morning. I bet he'll be glad to have me off his hands for a bit." Jack brushed his gloved hands on his coat and headed in through the heavy, wooden door that led into the back of the woodshop.

It wasn't but a few moments and Jack reappeared. "I'm all yours!" he said, and Ava was happy about it. She grabbed one of his hands and pulled him back to the street in front of the house.

"I've got something I need to show you," Ava said firmly. She wanted to say her intentions out loud so she couldn't back out.

They hurried through the streets until they were in front of Ava's house. Ava stared at it for a long while. Jack didn't make a sound. She'd always thought her house looked damaged after her father had died, as if the shingles hung a little more loosely and the siding sagged. For two years her mother had let the bushes out front grow wild, and the grass was unkempt, making their home appear to be abandoned. In truth, it had been abandoned by the person who had kept them knit together in happiness. However, as Ava looked at it now, the bushes and grass trimmed, it didn't seem so forlorn. It stood small, but mighty in its ability to withstand the storm that had passed over them in her father's death.

"I think the house could use a fresh coat of paint," Ava pondered.

"Is that what you have to show me?" Jack asked.

"No, it isn't, but promise me that you'll help me paint it this spring?" Ava looked at him seriously with a smile on her face.

"I, Jack, solemnly swear, that this spring you will find me outside your front door with a paintbrush in hand ready to bring new life onto the exterior of your home." Jack smiled back and gave a silly bow reminding Ava of her father and the games he would play with her.

Ava took a few steps up to her front door, turned to Jack, and said, "It's funny that you mention a paintbrush."

Jack followed her inside and they shrugged their winter gear off at the door, hanging them up carefully to dry. They then scrambled up the stairs until they found themselves in Ava's room. Ava took a deep breath.

"Before I show you, you must promise to keep this a secret between you and me. No one else would understand and I'm really hoping that you will," Ava said seriously.

"Another promise, Ava? You sure are demanding today." Jack's tone was playful, and he gave her a smirk so big it touched his eyes.

"I'm serious, Jack." She tried hard not to smile back. She knew the importance of the moment and wanted to be sure he did, too.

Jack changed his smirk to a genuine smile, "Of course, I promise."

"Close your eyes, please," Ava instructed. As soon as Jack had closed his eyes, she quietly knelt on the floor to take out her hidden paints, brushes, and paintings in the broken floorboard under her bed. She replaced the floorboard and gathered everything up to gently arrange it on her desk.

"Are you almost done?" Jack asked.

"Patience, Jack," Ava replied. She put the painting of the meadow and the painting of the winter wonderland side by side. Then she placed her brushes and paints above them. She took a deep breath and said, "Ready."

She watched him open his eyes adjusting to what had changed in the room.

I hope this was a good idea, her brain murmured.

A little faith, her heart replied.

Jack spotted the colors on her desk and slowly made his way to study them. For a while he didn't say anything. He just absorbed what was in front of him. Breathing was becoming hard for Ava. She wanted to know what was going on in his head.

"Did you paint these?" Jack asked in a whisper.

Ava nodded.

"Ava, these are…" Jack took a breath and picked up the winter wonderland studying it. "These are incredible. How long have you been painting? It must have taken years to become this good. These places feel so real."

"These are the first two I've painted," she said so quietly she swore she could hear the snow gently falling outside.

Jack turned to her with his eyes two sizes bigger than they were before. "These are the first two paintings you've ever created?"

Ava nodded once more. "I know it doesn't make sense, but that's not even the craziest part."

"There's more?" Jack asked.

"Jack, this next part is going to seem impossible. I didn't believe it myself at first. Everything I had known before made me believe what happened next couldn't be real. I sit down to paint and before I know it, the painting has created itself. I just have to think about it and somehow, I know what to do. It's like painting is part of me–as if I've been created to do it. But then, the painting becomes more." She paused, wanting to see how he was reacting to what she had already revealed.

She could tell he was trying to understand all she was saying. The look on his face was one that seemed as if he was thoughtfully processing. Seconds felt like minutes for Ava.

Finally, Jack said, "Okay. So, what's the impossible part?"

"I've been in these paintings. I've traveled through them."

9

She could feel Jack watching her intently as she sat in front of a fresh, new piece of paper. He was surprised when she'd told him about her trips through the paintings, but not suspicious of her sanity. Instead, he'd asked if she would show him how she painted. She understood his intrigue. It was something unusual. She would have been more skeptical than he was if he'd told her he'd traveled through paintings he perfectly painted on his first try.

"So, what's your process?" Jack asked gently. He was standing behind her, trying to give her space but she could feel his curiosity drawing him closer.

Ava thought for a second and then said, "I guess I just sit here while looking at my colors. I envision a place that seems beautiful and before I know it, I can feel it come to life. I look down and what was in my mind, is suddenly on my paper."

"That's incredible." Jack's voice was filled with wonder. "Where are you wanting to imagine today?"

Ava sorted through imagined scenery in her mind. She'd always wanted to hike to the top of a glorious mountain coated in fresh snow. She also would love to trek through the woods, exploring all the hidden places that were tucked within. A fall landscape would be breathtaking surrounded by the changing colors gesturing towards the end of a season and the beginning of a new one.

"There are so many places I'd love to paint," Ava said. "Where would you want to go if you could go anywhere, Jack?" She turned to see his face.

She watched as he thought intently as if he didn't want to give the wrong answer. Finally, he opened his mouth and said, "I've always wanted to feel the sand between my toes and look out over a vast ocean. I've heard of oceans. The blue of it is unlike any other blue. I don't know what it would smell like, but I imagine it smells different—refreshing."

"Then that's what I'll paint," Ava declared. She dipped her paintbrush in the water and began the process.

The empty page soon became full of color. Ava felt a gust of salty air whip through her hair, and she smiled to herself as a tiny, blue crab scrambled across the beach of plush sand she had effortlessly created in front of a large expanse of ocean blue. She'd forgotten that Jack was standing behind her, being swept up in the magic of what happened between her and the paintbrush.

"I don't know what to say," Jack let out an almost inaudible whisper.

Ava wondered if he had seen the tiny blue crab move, too.

"What do you see?" Ava asked.

After several moments passed, Jack gathered up his words and said, "I feel like I've been there before. It's as if you painted the perfect beach that exists in only the best places."

Ava took a deep breath, "Did you see the tiny, blue crab?" She looked up at Jack, now standing beside her. He shook his head. "Come closer. Really focus."

Ava scooted over so Jack could sit on the tiny, wooden chair with her. Ava, once again, felt the ocean breeze and the ocean slowly began to move in an enchanting sway. This time she caught a glimmer in the sand and a beautiful, pink seashell came alive in front of her.

"How is this real?" Jack murmured as he grabbed Ava's hand.

"You can see it all?" Ava excitedly replied as she squeezed Jack's hand. She broke her gaze from the painting to catch Jack nodding.

"Now what happens?" he asked.

"I've never traveled with anyone through the paintings, but you must believe it is possible. Do you believe we can, Jack?" She questioned while smiling at him, a sparkle in her eyes.

"I do." He finally broke his own gaze from the painting and met Ava's stare.

"We'll look back into the painting and then close our eyes. Don't let go of me, just in case." Ava was filled with a rush of eagerness at the possibility that Jack would get to experience being in one of her paintings with her. Would the man appear? Would Jack be able to go through?

"Okay." He nodded at Ava, and she could feel his mix of nervousness and possibility.

They both looked back at the painting.

Ava counted, "Close your eyes in one...two...three..."

For a quick second, she wondered if Jack would be there when she opened her eyes, but she quickly shoved the thought away. She didn't want to give any room to doubt. She allowed hope to bloom in her chest. She believed with all she had that her and Jack would open their eyes looking over the ocean with their feet buried deep into the soft sand.

Ava smelt the salt that was thick in the air before she opened her eyes, and she knew she was there. She could still feel the warmth of

Jack's hand in hers. She opened her eyes quickly and squealed when she saw him beside her, standing with his eyes closed.

"Jack! Jack! We're here!" Ava couldn't bottle up her delight, it spilled over her face and made its way into her voice as she erupted in laughter.

Jack opened his eyes but was silent. Ava danced in the sand around him. The sand between her toes felt like velvet, it was so deliciously soft. The air was slightly sticky with salt, but made her mind feel clear and sharp. The sound of the ocean was beyond any other soothing sound she'd ever heard. It was gentle, but strong and reminded Ava of her father.

"Jack. Are you okay?" Ava stood in front of him, Jack unmoving.

"I don't have any words." Jack sighed, wonderment coating his exhale.

"That is saying a lot for you, Jack. You are always the one with the words," Ava giggled. She grabbed both of Jack's hands. "Wiggle your toes, Jack. Take a deep breath and smell the ocean."

Jack did as he was told, and Ava watched pure joy slowly wash over him until he was glowing like the scenery around them.

"What are we wearing?" Jack suddenly questioned.

Ava looked down and saw she was in a bright pink dress that had tiny white flowers sprinkled all over it. The material felt different, like it would dry quickly. She looked over at Jack and he was wearing a blue and white striped outfit that seemed to be made of the same fabric.

"I think these are swim clothes," Ava said with a smile. "Every time I go through a painting, I'm dressed in the most colorful, wonderful things that go perfectly with where I am."

"I've never worn blue before," Jack said. It was a simple statement but one that Ava felt deeply. She'd enjoyed the beautiful outfits and wished that she could wear such things in Dryden. No one wore color. She'd never even seen fabric with any vibrancy sold in any of the stores.

"You know what this means though?" Ava opened her eyes wide. "We can go swim in the ocean!"

Before she could run off with hope that Jack would be quick behind her, a familiar voice interrupted their conversation, "Hello, Avisha. Hello, Jack."

She turned and there was the man. She had wondered if he would show up. Jack turned towards the man, too, surprise flickering on his face.

"How did you know my name?" Jack asked.

"I've always known you. It's wonderful to see that Avisha is sharing her gift with you." The man's voice was comforting and filled with assurance that Ava had made the right decision in bringing Jack through the painting.

"But I've never met you before." Jack wasn't happy with the man's answer and Ava could see the perplexed look on Jack's face grow.

"You have, Jack. It's just you've never put a face with who you've met." The man smiled at Jack. "So, what brings you two to the beach today?"

Ava smiled, "I let Jack choose where I painted today." Suddenly, Ava realized she'd never told the man she had painted the places in which she arrived. He had mentioned to Jack he was glad she was sharing her gift. Was he talking about her painting?

"I see you are confused alongside your friend today, Avisha. Are you wondering how I knew you had a special talent?" The man smiled at her through his eyes.

Ava nodded.

"I know you well, Avisha. I know how many hairs are on your head. I know that your father's laugh was your favorite sound in the world. I know you desire to wear a pretty, bright dress. I know about the cracked mirror with the reflection that becomes more vibrant with every trip you take through a painting that you painted yourself. It's a beautiful talent, Avisha. One that can show the world just how incredible this place is. I'm so glad your mother helped you discover it."

Ava digested everything the man had just told her and if anyone else would have said these things, she may have been frightened they knew so much that she hadn't shared with them, but this man had always seemed different. He never seemed like he was the same as everyone else from Dryden. He'd always felt as if he was the source of comfort and peace. She never felt like she should fear his presence or his knowledge.

"Do you think my mother knew she gave me what I needed?" Ava asked the man.

"I think your mother knows you are special and wanted to give you something as special as you are," the man replied. "Maybe she didn't know about your talent, but she may have known it would be something that would help you create the beauty you desired in the world."

Ava thought about what he said and believed that to be true. She didn't think her mother knew how easy the painting came to her or how it allowed her to exist in a completely different place, but she did think her mother wanted her to create something colorful in her life.

Then Jack spoke up, "Who are you?"

"Jack, I know you just as well as I know Avisha. You find the brightness in every moment, even when no one else can see it. You work hard, hoping one day your father will see how much you care.

You give people so much grace, even when it isn't deserved. You also have a talent that I believe you've discovered?" The man had turned to Jack with a tender face and spoke the words with such gentleness that Ava was sure Jack felt how genuine and compassionate this man really was.

"I can write," Jack said quietly.

"You don't just write, Jack. You create the most beautiful stories and places with your words. It's a wonderful gift. One that can connect people in a way others cannot."

"But writing about things that aren't factual in Dryden is frowned upon. People don't like when others try to find a voice that doesn't fit with what they expect from you." Jack's voice was so soft that Ava could barely hear him. Jack's usual confidence had diminished and been replaced with a sadness that concerned Ava.

The man took Jack by the shoulders softly, squaring him up so Jack would listen fully, and then said, "Jack. You were not created to please other people. People are fickle, allowing their feelings to foolishly guide them. There will always be people who don't choose to see the good in you. You should never make yourself less because it might scare others."

"I don't think I scare them," Jack said.

"You scare them more than you know. They wouldn't try to mold you into a version they approve of if you didn't scare them," the man replied.

Jack was quiet. Ava was quiet, too.

"I think it's time we played in the ocean. You are wearing perfectly good swim clothes and we can't let that go to waste." The man smiled at them both extending a hand to each child. Ava and Jack grabbed on. "Let's not worry about what we've kept hidden for fear of what others might think. Let's just embrace the beauty that is in front of us."

Their steps towards the ocean were timid, their minds still processing what the man had said. Soon, the heaviness disappeared as the water splashed over their bodies as if it were washing away the expectations that had weighed heavy on them both. Soon, they all were laughing as the waves crashed over them leaving behind drenched hair and salty skin.

"There's nothing like being washed clean," the man said.

And Ava agreed. The ocean felt like magic, just like the snow had. The longer she was in the water, the more energetic and confident she felt. She hoped Jack felt it, too.

10

When she opened her eyes, they were back in her room. Ava felt the chill in the air from winter in Dryden. It was a stark difference from the beach they had just been playing on. They were still sitting side by side in the small, wooden chair, hands clutched together. The painting was in front of them, and Ava had to squint, but she saw three pairs of footprints pressed lightly in the sand.

"That was…" Jack's voice began but then trailed off.

"I know. My brain has been trying to process how this can be real, but I'm beginning to think that maybe all things don't have to make sense from our own understanding." Ava realized she probably was overexplaining to Jack, but she was nervous he thought she was strange or possibly losing her mind.

"That isn't what I was going to say," Jack began. "That was incredible. It was beyond anything I believed was possible. I'm going to replay what happened repeatedly in my head for days. No, years. Probably all my life. There was something familiar and yet surreal about that place. And that man. He kept insisting he knew me and that I knew him, and for some reason I felt he was telling the truth. But I've never seen the man."

"It's fascinating, isn't it? I have thought the same thing. I have never seen the man and yet, I feel like I've known him my entire life." Ava was so excited to have someone else to talk to about her paintings, and then she realized she didn't know what time it was. She needed to run to the butcher. She scrambled up from the chair dropping Jack's hand and ran to the window. The sun was still in the sky, but it was making its way down to the earth.

"I need to get to the butcher today!" she exclaimed. She ran out of her room and down the stairs with Jack following behind her. She grabbed the coins on the table and hurried to put her winter coat and gloves on before slipping her feet into her boots.

Ava was so focused on rushing out the door she startled when Jack grabbed her by the shoulders. "Ava, thank you. Thank you for sharing what you did with me today. I know it couldn't have been easy, but it was something I'll never forget. You have a gift and for what it's worth, I love it."

She needed those words from Jack. She was right to trust him with her secret. Ava's arms flew around his neck, and she gave him a forceful hug that made him stumble backwards.

"I have to go," she muttered into the thickness of Jack's coat trying to hold back the waterfall of tears that were wanting to burst from behind her eyelids. Ava took a deep breath, let go of Jack, and ran off towards the butcher shop.

Ava was able to collect herself as she walked the streets and managed to only let one teardrop fall which she quickly wiped away with her scratchy, gloved hand. Her boots sloshed through the snow that was turning to mush, reminding Ava that winter break was coming to an end. She reached the butcher shop and noticed that the faded, front door had a hint of red to it, something she'd never noticed before. Then Ava looked down the street and noticed a whisper of color over the entire town.

She opened the door and a loud, out-of-tune clang sounded alerting the butcher of her arrival.

"Good afternoon, Mr. Kellogg." Ava shook the chill from her as she welcomed the warmth of the butcher's shop. "I love your red door."

Mr. Kellogg looked at her perplexed. "What can I get for you today, Miss Ava?"

Ava had always loved Mr. Kellogg. He didn't seem as gruff as a butcher could be and she always thought he wasn't as sensitive to the rules and expectations of Dryden. One time, he'd even smiled at her—a rare sight from an adult.

"What's on special, Mr. Kellogg?" Ava asked, rubbing the silver coins together in her coat pocket.

"Pork chops," he replied.

"I'll take two, please." Ava smiled as she took the coins out of her pocket and placed them on the counter. "Mr. Kellogg, can I ask you a question?"

Mr. Kellogg took the coins off the counter, opened his register, and they made a happy sound as they joined the rest of the coins inside. He then looked at Ava and nodded, not saying a word.

"When did you stop believing?" Ava asked the question boldly. Maybe it was the fact that she saw Dryden was becoming a world of pastels instead of grays, or maybe it was the journey to the beach with Jack, but she felt inspired to figure out why the people had lost their hope.

Mr. Kellogg's expression turned soft for a second. Ava caught the glaze that blanketed over his eyes and the way his face fell gently, but then watched as he tightened his brow and blinked to make his eyes go dry. "That isn't a question a young lady like yourself should be asking." His lips tightened as the words squeezed through.

Ava shrugged her shoulders. "It just seems to me that there is a little more to see than what everyone is looking for. Before coming into your shop, I noticed a color beginning to bloom over the buildings. It wasn't there a few weeks ago. At least, I didn't see it a few weeks ago."

Mr. Kellogg seemed to wince at her words but managed to say, "That is the kind of thinking that will get you in trouble around here, Miss Ava. Your mind must be playing games with you. There isn't anything special happening here in Dryden."

She knew Mr. Kellogg was trying to help, even if it wasn't helpful at all. She began to realize that the man in the paintings might be right. She could feel the fear that had overcome Mr. Kellogg with her questioning. She wondered what could be so scary about believing there was something more and why grown adults could be so scared of a child looking for it.

"You can go ahead and wrap up my pork chops, Mr. Kellogg, but I also think you are wrong. I think something special is happening. Everyone has just become blind to it."

Mr. Kellogg didn't say another word as he wrapped two pork chops up in brown paper and string. As he handed them over the counter to Ava, he avoided looking into her eyes.

How peculiar that he seems so afraid, her brain said.

Ava agreed with her brain. Something seemed very off about this encounter which only made her more intrigued by what it could be.

"Thank you so much, Mr. Kellogg. I truly hope you have a wonderful rest of your day." Ava smiled brightly at him and then turned on her heels to head out the door.

But she stopped suddenly when she heard him speak quietly, "Just so you know, Ava, your father was a good man. He didn't deserve what happened to him, but you must be careful with your thinking around here. There are a lot of people that won't like the questions you have to ask."

Ava turned around slowly and swallowed deeply before she said, "When you say he didn't deserve what happened to him, do you mean the sickness that took him or the streets that were torn apart because he chose to dance in them?"

She saw Mr. Kellogg wince once more.

"He didn't deserve any of it." Mr. Kellogg's eyes fell downward as he admitted to what Ava said.

Ava walked a few steps back to the counter and said, "You know, Mr. Kellogg, I've been thinking about my father a lot lately. He had every reason to be angry, but he didn't choose to be. Why do you think that is?"

Mr. Kellogg didn't look up as he said, "I don't know."

"I think he knew something that everyone else didn't and I'm going to figure out what that something was. I would much rather be like my father than to be drained of color like the rest of Dryden." Ava felt confidence rise in her chest as she said the words and, in that moment, she realized how true they were. She did want to be more like her father. She wanted to choose to hope. Maybe her father wasn't there to help her, but he'd lived a life that left a light in her heart.

With that realization, she spun back around, and left the butcher shop for home. She had a new determination within her that she hoped would lead her to the answers she sought.

11

Ava stared up at the bell nestled on top of the schoolhouse. Winter break had concluded, and it was time to attend classes once again. Her nerves were bouncing within her body, making every muscle feel tense. She knew she had changed over break, and she feared being molded back to the version of her that clung to melancholy like it was the most magical part of her she had.

The man had warned her that once she showed her light to the world, others would attempt to snuff it out. She'd taken another journey through a painting before break was over. It was a peaceful landscape that included a vast field of red poppies. Their petals were delicate and soft. She'd picked one and placed it behind her ear. She'd worn a dress in the shade of a tender blue with a scalloped edging that peeked out from under puffed sleeves. Her feet were wrapped in crimson, silk slippers that matched the poppies. She had wished she could appear back in her room wearing the dress and the slippers.

The poppy fields had been surrounded by dense woods painted in dark greens and blacks, but the darkness wasn't the kind that felt like it held a frightening mystery, but one that held lost secrets. The man had soon appeared beside her, greeting Ava the same as he always did.

He'd taken her hand and they'd walked through the field towards the dark forest. As they made their way into the trees, Ava looked up to the tops of their branches. The light broke through above, sending a muted light to guide their path forward.

"Beautiful, isn't it?" the man had asked. "The way the light can be seen even in the darkest of places?"

She had agreed. She loved the way the light could change the way the forest looked. She imagined without light the woods would appear colorless. The light allowed her to see the different shades of green and even discover different flowers that grew on the forest floor. It made her think about the color she had seen on the buildings in Dryden. They were faint, but they were there.

"I have something strange to ask," Ava had said to the man.

The man had stopped, light dancing on his face from the sun streaming through. "You can ask me anything, Avisha," he had said.

"When I go back home after being in a painting, the world around me seems different."

The man had smiled at her and asked, "Different, how?"

"It seems more colorful. Dryden has always lacked color, everything coated in shades of gray. But each time I go back home, things become more vibrant. Last time, I saw the faint hint of red in a door and then noticed pastel shades of color on all the buildings down the street. When I look at myself in the mirror, my hair looks more yellow and my eyes greener. I even have pink cheeks."

"So, what is your question?"

"How is that possible?" Her question had been bold, no longer shy in her conversations with this man she felt she had always known.

"Maybe you've become like the light through the trees." He had pointed up and Ava had looked at the beams that highlighted color all around her.

"Me, a light?" Ava had questioned.

"Where there is light, there is color. Where there is darkness, it is hidden," he had simply said.

"But how am I a light?" Ava had scrunched up her face in confusion.

"Light can come from people, too. It's not just found in the sun, the moon, or the stars. People can brighten up the world or they can cast shadows through their own pity. Maybe you are seeing more color because you have decided to look for what is good?"

She had pondered the explanation and begun to realize the truth that matched his words. Every time she had come home from traveling through a painting, she had wanted to believe there was more around her than what she had seen before. She had begun to hope for more and not just hope for it, but believe it was there.

"Avisha, being a light is a beautiful thing in a world that needs it, but where there is light, there will also be people who want to extinguish it. Be careful of those that want to snuff it out."

It had been a warning and standing in front of the school, she now knew the weight of the words he had given her. She worried what others would think of her, and how they would react. She felt someone standing beside her and turned to see Jack.

"Hey, Ava." He gave her a smile and nudged her shoulder.

"Hi, Jack." She took a big, audible breath through her nose and exhaled.

"You seem worried." Concern flashed over Jack's face.

"Jack, do you see color?" Ava asked.

"What do you mean?" He looked at her confused.

"When you look at the buildings in Dryden are they muted shades of gray or are they colorful?"

"They've always been colored in the faintest of shades, but they've become a little more vibrant lately." He took her hand and squeezed it. "What about you?"

Ava took a deep breath again, "I used to look at everything and see the world drained of color. Everything looked plain and boring. When my mother gave me the paints, I'd never seen so much color in all my life until I used them to paint. But then it wasn't just the paintings that were colorful, the world here in Dryden started to change as I changed."

Jack gave her hand another squeeze, "That's beautiful, Ava."

She looked at the schoolhouse and said, "I'm worried that the changes in me won't be enough."

"Enough for what?"

"Enough to keep me from going back to how I was. What if others try to hurt me?" The nerves within Ava kept rattling. She watched as other kids slowly shuffled into the building. For the first time she noticed the different colors of their hair hidden under plain caps. Shades of yellow and red were mixed in with the browns and blacks.

"I just want everyone to see the world around them like I've begun to see it," she whispered.

"So, let's show them," Jack said, and he pulled Ava with him into the schoolhouse.

Class began and the studies felt repetitive. Mrs. Polly must have felt they would forget all they learned over break and had decided they'd repeat lessons they'd already learned. Without lessons that forced her brain to work, her brain had time to worry.

No one will notice you are different if you don't show it, her brain told her.

But Ava wanted to be different, she didn't want to hide how she had changed. Math facts turned into handwriting practice to ensure their cursive was precise. Her hand cramped at the tedious task. She looked up at Jack sitting across the aisle on the boy's side.

Jack had already completed every writing worksheet and they looked perfect from Ava's viewpoint. Then she remembered his gift of writing. His hand was probably skillfully trained from long hours of secret practice. He was sitting quietly with his hands resting behind his head as he watched everyone else completing their lessons. She caught Mrs. Polly giving him a disapproving look at the fact he had completed so early. It set him apart, showing that his handwriting skills were better than others.

Mrs. Polly got up from her desk, grabbed another worksheet, and placed it in front of Jack.

"Why thank you, Mrs. Polly." Jack dared to smile.

It caught Mrs. Polly off guard. No one had smiled or expressed any notion of happiness in the classroom for a very long time. Mrs. Polly began to open her mouth, but no words came out, so she chose to ignore the smile and returned to her desk.

Ava was thankful when Mrs. Polly finally dismissed class for lunch. She hurried and grabbed her lunch sack and ran outside to her favorite spot, a dead log that rested underneath a tree that was still bare from winter. She sat and stared up at the branches and noticed little green buds waiting for their turn to grow.

Seconds later, Jack joined her.

"I wasn't sure what Mrs. Polly was going to do when you smiled at her," Ava said with a slight grin.

Jack began to unpack his sandwich and said, "I just wanted to see how she'd react. Then she didn't do anything. It makes you wonder if the expectations in Dryden are actual rules or if we've all just been trained to believe they are."

Ava pondered this and it made sense. Ava had never seen a list of rules that prohibited the things people disapproved of. It was possible that over time, expectations had become things people believed were rules to abide by.

"It makes you wonder about the history of Dryden. The history we haven't been taught," Ava said.

"I've told you that Dryden wasn't always this way," Jack answered.

"But how do we learn more?" Ava asked.

They both sat in silence eating their lunches of sandwiches and oranges. The oranges were beautiful to Ava—a bright orange against the dead of winter. Soon they heard Mrs. Polly calling for the children to head back inside to complete the rest of their school day.

"Can you meet after school?" Jack turned to Ava. "I may have an idea."

Ava didn't know where to start with trying to uncover the history of Dryden, so she was thankful Jack had a plan. There had to be more to this story, and she was hoping they could figure it out.

12

The school day was finally over and Ava was relieved. Jack had proved his skills in writing were developing when he finished their vocabulary and spelling lessons quickly. He had smiled at Mrs. Polly again, and she hadn't even paused to think about responding. She had ignored him completely, which didn't feel like defeat to Ava or Jack. Instead, it made them even more curious.

"What's the plan?" Ava asked.

"I think I know someone who might be willing to help us," Jack said in a hushed tone. "But we will need to be careful. Revealing Dryden's real history isn't something most people want around here; otherwise, it wouldn't be hidden from us."

She knew Jack was right. Whatever had been hidden was hidden for a reason.

Jack led her through the streets of Dryden before they slid into a back alley.

"Is it really necessary to go in the back way?" Ava's eyebrows lifted. "I don't think anyone is suspicious of us yet."

"It isn't for our safety. I want to make sure we protect the person who I think will help us," Jack replied.

Jack walked silently through the alley and Ava followed. He stopped at a narrow wooden door that seemed grayer from years of weathering than the beautiful, rich brown it had probably once been. Jack took another look around them before reaching for the rusted doorknob.

"Where are we?" Ava whispered, unable to tell which storefront was on the other side from the alley.

"It's the bookstore," Jack said. He slipped through the slender gap effortlessly, as if he'd done it many times before.

Ava followed, but she closed her eyes and sucked in her breath as she slid through, imagining the doorframe would turn to teeth and eat her right up. Her eyes adjusted to the complete blackness of the small, cold room they'd snuck into. She wasn't sure how, but she felt an icy edge that hadn't pierced her in the bitterness outside. As the room began to develop out of its dark fog, she saw a small desk and a metal chair that had rusted over time. Otherwise, the room appeared to be bare in its smallness. She noticed another narrow door that she figured led to the bookstore.

This seems like a bad idea, her brain piped up.

She agreed and didn't fight the thought. Something felt desolate and yet, dangerous, too. Even her heart had picked up its beat in anticipation of what would happen next. She hadn't been to the bookstore in years as it was void of anything she cared to read. It was filled with a thoroughly inspected collection of books that were considered acceptable for the people of Dryden. All the covers were black, with no color to be seen. The text was plain and boring—the content even more so.

"Have you been here before?" Ava grabbed Jack's arm and clung to it as she said the words.

"Maybe," Jack said as he gave her a slightly mischievous grin.

"Then why do you seem so scared?" Ava questioned.

"Because I'm not entirely sure the answer is here, or that Ms. Beckett is willing to help us." Jack sighed and turned to face Ava fully. "I've been here many times. Ms. Beckett knows I write, but the books we are allowed to have in Dryden do not contain the inspiration my heart yearns for. I come through that back door often, sit at that metal chair, and devour novels in vibrant colors with beautiful fonts that take me places I've never heard about or have even known to dream about. If someone knows about any books that contain the real history of Dryden, it must be Ms. Beckett."

Ava's mind swayed. Jack's secret held more details than just his skills in writing, and now he had just shared it with her. It was a secret that also existed in the feeling that there had to be something more.

"Jack, why do you think they keep so much from us?"

Jack took a deep breath and moments passed until he finally spoke up, "I don't know for sure, Ava, but I think the man in your painting was right when he said they are scared. I don't know what they fear, but those who choose fear often lose their faith."

They stood there for a while. Ava was pondering what Jack had said. It was puzzling why such wonderful things like her painting and Jack's writing had to stay hidden. Then suddenly, the narrow door that led to the bookstore swung open.

There was an immediate shock in Ms. Beckett's eyes at the sight of Ava there with Jack. Ms. Beckett nervously looked over at Jack and raised her fuzzy eyebrows.

"Hello again, Ms. Beckett. I hope you don't mind but I've brought my friend, Ava, today. I don't feel I can share with you exactly why Ava is here, except we both are hoping you can help us." Jack's voice was calm and steady, and it put Ava at ease. She had worried that Ms. Beckett may push them back through the alley door, never allowing Jack back in.

"I paint!" Ava blurted out. Ava's eyes grew wide, and she bit her lip hoping Ms. Beckett would take her secret and keep it with the fragility it deserved.

Ms. Beckett's face became soft, and a tiny smile bloomed upon her lips. She nodded gently before taking a few steps towards Ava and gathering Ava up in her arms. It was a warm hug—a hug that traveled all the way to Ava's toes that finally relaxed in her stiff, black boots. People in Dryden didn't hug and now Ava knew why. It seemed to be a gesture of acceptance and love, something that could inspire others to believe in something more.

"Oh, dear girl! You paint!" Ms. Beckett exclaimed. "Painting is such a magical gift! I haven't seen a fresh painting in so long."

Ava's eyebrows raised as she said, "A fresh painting?"

Ms. Beckett winked. "I'm sure Jack has told you of the novels he eats up faster than a child with a forbidden sack of candy. Books aren't the only thing I have that possess color, beauty, and hope."

Ava's heart raced so quickly that she was sure Ms. Beckett and Jack could hear the hum of it. "You have paintings?"

The question came out like a gentle breeze from her mouth, softer than a whisper. Ava had never seen any other painting than her own. She hadn't been sure if there were any in Dryden.

"I do," Ms. Beckett beamed. "But did I hear right when I heard you say you had a question?"

Ms. Beckett turned to Jack.

"We are hoping you can help us." Jack took a deep breath. "We want to know more about the history of Dryden. The real history. Not the history we've been told in school."

Ms. Beckett's expression didn't change at first. She looked between both Ava and Jack. Ava took this time to study Ms. Beckett. Ms. Beckett had beautiful, copper hair that was pulled loosely back in a bun. Spirals of hair fell around her face, framing the plumpness of it. Ava noticed laugh lines indented around Ms. Beckett's eyes, which would have confused Ava if she hadn't heard Ms. Beckett's bubbly laugh whistle through her ears as she had wrapped her strong arms around Ava's body in a hug just moments before. Ms. Beckett had a life of laughter, whether it was something the people of Dryden approved of or not. The evidence was marked on her face and Ava was happy for it.

Finally, Ms. Beckett spoke, "There is great responsibility in the knowledge in which you seek. I know you both have questions, but I'm worried what you discover may be too heavy of a weight to bear. Once you know the truth, it's hard to keep it quiet."

"But you are able to keep it quiet," Jack said.

Ms. Beckett's eyes became sad, and she replied, "I keep it from those who seek to destroy it. If some people knew I held evidence of truth, I'm sure I would discover my bookstore burnt to ash some morning."

The grief in Ms. Beckett's voice was one that had seen others hurt at the hands of those who want to destroy the truth. It reminded Ava of her mother's sadness when she had told her about the streets being turned to rubble.

"Ms. Beckett, did you know my father?" Ava asked.

"Oh, yes." Ms. Beckett's sadness turned back to a smile. "He was such a joyful man. I am so sorry you live a life without him, Ava. His dancing always made me laugh."

"Do you know who destroyed the streets of Dryden?"

Ava's next question brought Ms. Beckett's sorrow back. Jack looked at Ava confused. She hadn't told Jack about the streets being destroyed as an attempt to steal the joy from her father.

"Ava, sometimes we wish to know who did such terrible things believing the knowledge of it will heal the hurt, but that's not always true. The important thing you need to hold onto is that your father never let other people define him. He still smiled. He still laughed. He still found joy. Joy isn't dependent on circumstances, Ava. Your father knew that." Ms. Beckett said the words as her eyes glazed over with salty tears. She didn't try to wipe them away. She just let them fall down her rosy cheeks.

This time Ava walked to Ms. Beckett and carefully placed her arms around the woman. It had been so long since she had hugged someone other than her mother or Jack. Ms. Beckett fell into Ava, taking any comfort Ava had to give her.

Jack stood still until Ms. Beckett registered the confusion on his face and looked down at Ava mirroring Jack's confusion.

"He doesn't know," Ava said, answering the question she knew Ms. Beckett had.

"There is much you both do not know." Ms. Beckett backed away from Ava. "I can show you what you are looking for, but you will have to figure out if you are prepared for it. You'll have to be honest with yourselves. I cannot know what you are ready for, only you can."

Ms. Beckett walked over to a corner in the room and bent over, placing her fingers in a slightly larger gap in the floorboards. She pulled up and a large door opened from beneath. Ava gasped.

Ms. Beckett smiled at them both, "Ready, or not?"

13

They sat in the basement of the bookstore digging through old, wooden boxes filled with the most colorful books Ava had ever seen. She'd been distracted multiple times already, getting lost in the descriptions of far-off places and daring characters that ran after danger courageously.

"So, you paint?" Ms. Beckett looked up from a book that was bound in a rich green leather. The words were inscribed on the spine in a vibrant gold.

"I do," Ava said, not looking up from the story she'd begun to devour. It was a story about a princess with bold, red hair. She sought a buried treasure that was said to hold the key to peace, something the princess's kingdom desperately needed. Ava was mesmerized by the vivid descriptions.

"How long have you been painting?" Ms. Beckett continued her questions.

"Not long. I've only painted a few pieces." Ava still didn't look up. She also didn't notice the silence that hung in the air around them as Ms. Beckett shot Jack a look that prodded him to add to Ava's reply.

"She's amazing. I've watched her paint. It's like the paint brush is an extension of her. The paint comes to life in the most beautiful scenery."

"So, you have a gift," Ms. Beckett stated and her statement broke Ava's trance from the story in her lap. She looked at Ms. Beckett as she continued, "A gift is different than a skill. Anyone can paint, or write, or dance, or sing but those that can do something as if it comes from the very core of who they are...that's a gift. If it feels like it is part of you, that's a gift. If it fills your lungs with an energy that excites you, that's a gift. So, does it?"

Ava thought about how she felt when she painted. She thought about how she could feel the scenery before it became reality on her paper. She thought about how she could smell the flowers or taste the snow upon her tongue, a reality all her own while in the process of creating.

"The paintings feel like they are part of me. I don't understand it, but it instantly felt like I was made to paint," Ava finally replied.

Ms. Beckett beamed. "This is exciting! The potential within both of you is incredible. Not everyone recognizes their gifts, or when they do, they doubt themselves and then hide it from the world."

"But we do have to hide it from the people in Dryden," Ava stated.

Ms. Beckett reached over and took one of Ava's hands and squeezed. "I have this hope that things are about to change. I can feel it."

Ava wanted to believe her, but how could she say that? They were currently sitting in a dark, musty basement full of wonder and beauty that was hidden from Dryden because if it was found, it would be destroyed.

"You doubt it will change?" Ms. Beckett asked Ava.

"If our gifts are so great, I don't get why people won't accept them," Ava said dryly. Their quest felt more impossible than the quest she had begun to read in the fairytale.

"I don't have all the answers in case you thought I would be the one that holds them. I believe you may know who does though. However, I do know that for change to happen, people must change first. I believe that is happening in both of you." Ms. Beckett smiled and then resumed going through her crate of books.

But how can two kids change a whole town? Ava's brain and heart felt in sync with this question, and she wondered the same. She also wondered what Ms. Beckett had meant when she said Ava already knew who held the answers. The deeper they dove into what Ava hoped would give them answers, the more questions she had.

"What are we looking for?" Jack interrupted her thoughts.

"There is a box in here that contains a set of the old, history books they once taught from in Dryden. I believe they are yellow, but it has been so long since I've seen them. I've kept them tucked away and cannot recall their exactness," Ms. Beckett answered.

"Ms. Beckett," Ava began, "What happens when we find these books?"

Ms. Beckett closed the top on the crate she had dug through and said, "That will be up to you two."

"How will we know what to do?" Jack asked, a flicker of worry on his face.

Ms. Beckett shrugged her shoulders and replied, "I don't have an answer for that. Sometimes we just know when the moment comes."

They continued digging through boxes and crates silently. Ava's mind was filled with nervousness, the smell of the old books clouding her mind with anxiousness of what they might find. Just as Ms. Beckett had warned them, she felt the heaviness of responsibility beginning to sit on her shoulders. If they decided to know, they couldn't ever go back to not knowing. Would they be able to live with the truth in what they discovered if they found it?

Ava heard Jack gasp and she flung herself around to look in his direction. In the dusty crate in front of him she saw the glow of yellow.

"I think I found them," Jack mumbled as he carefully picked up the book sitting on top. Ava scrambled to his side. The lettering was faint, a worn metallic silver that seemed to smudge into the faded yellow of the book's linen cover.

The History of First Springs

"This isn't them," Ava said with sureness. "I've never even heard of First Springs."

Ms. Beckett looked at both Jack and Ava with a tenderness that made Ava question how confident her answer had been. "Dryden hasn't always been Dryden," she said quietly.

Ava shook her head, "I don't understand."

"There should be eight volumes in that crate. The very last one details the change of names that happened with the change of times." Ms. Beckett kept her quiet tone. "I'll leave you two to decide what you are to do next."

Ava and Jack kept silent as Ms. Beckett climbed the creaky stairs back up to the main floor of the bookstore. Ava felt dizzy, her focus twirling in grand circles until Jack took her hand jolting her back into the present.

"We don't have to know," Jack said. "We can put these books away forever and vow to never open them."

Ava knew that wasn't an option. She shook her head as she said, "We can't, Jack. We know the truth exists in these books. Avoiding the truth doesn't make it less true. Avoiding the truth when you know you can have it is much worse than never knowing there was a truth to know at all."

"Do you regret looking for the truth, Ava?" Jack muttered. "It may have been easier to never have known these existed."

"We're about to find out, aren't we?" Ava sighed as she squeezed Jack's hand. "Besides, would we ever be truly happy not knowing the truth?"

Jack squeezed her hand back, "Where's the adventure in that?"

They decided to start with the first volume after debating if they should skip ahead to the last volume to see why First Springs had changed its name to Dryden. They had finally decided they'd rather know the origin story first and if they felt it was necessary, they would open the eighth volume leaving the other six unexplored.

Jack held the first volume in his lap and asked, "Are you ready?"

Ava smiled at him with hope that what they would discover would be worth the weight of the knowledge, and said, "I'm ready."

But Ava wasn't as ready as she'd thought. When Jack opened the book, the first page contained a painting. It was an exact replica of the first painting she'd ever created.

14

Ava had sat frozen in shock; she couldn't even force herself to blink.

"Ava!" Jack had said as he had shaken her. "Ava! Are you okay?"

Finally, Ava had been able to shake herself free from the state of disbelief.

"I'm okay," she had managed.

Then Jack had read the caption below the painting.

The place where the Living Water flows.

Ava hadn't understood. She'd been there—she'd traveled through her painting to that place. There was no town there. It had been the most wonderous field with a glow that gave it the most vibrant colors. Nothing that resembled a version of Dryden had existed in that field.

The first pages had been filled with a story that sounded more like a fairytale than real life. It was a creation story of grand imagination. It detailed out an abundance of color and life. People were joyful and Ava had felt laughter rippling off the pages as they had absorbed the history that laid before them. The pages had even seemed to glisten after years of being forgotten, as if they were brightly sparkling out of excitement from being discovered.

It seemed impossible that what they read was the beginning of Dryden. What could have happened that created the Dryden that Jack and she knew?

Ms. Beckett had retrieved them when the sun started fading along with the day and she knew they best get home. They'd carefully put the book back in the crate and closed it up, promising Ms. Beckett they'd be back another day.

They'd walked home in silence, digesting all the new information they'd just discovered, but now Ava was sitting at her desk with a fresh sheet of paper in front of her and her colors laid out.

Ava's brain had been stunned seeing a duplicate painting of hers in an ancient, history book. She didn't want to admit it to Jack right away, but it made her begin to doubt what she was capable of with her own painting. If it had already been done, what good was her own gift?

Is your painting good enough? her brain finally asked. She felt her heart flutter at her brain's question as if had the same uncertainty.

Ava sat unmoving, staring at the blank page. She was filled with hesitation and now, doubt. It may have just been a coincidence that the first three paintings seemed perfect, and Jack was so kind that he would never have told her they weren't as magical as she believed.

"I don't know if I can do this," she whispered to nobody.

She began picking up her supplies and she placed them back in their hiding place. She crawled into her bed, burying herself under the blankets. Doubts began to swirl within her, making her stomach feel queasy. A tear slid down her cheek, followed by several more. She let them fall, soaking her pillow in her fear of inadequacy. She fell asleep drowning in her cries that filled her body with a dread she knew well. The dread that made her feel as if she were ordinary, not truly meant for something more.

15

The smell of buttery rolls drifted up the staircase as she heard her mother shouting, "Ava! Jack is here!"

The darkness mixed with a faint sunrise out her window. Ava had just pulled her hair back, forgoing the ribbon she'd been saving to wear for a day she felt bold enough to add a little frill to her plain clothes. This morning was not a day she felt brave. Her eyes were as puffy as the pillow she had cried into all night.

Her reflection seemed to taunt her as she felt drained of color, nothing as vibrant as it was the day before. Melancholy draped over her shoulders, and she wore it like the comfort of an old friend.

"Coming!" She glanced toward her bedroom door and replied with dread. She knew Jack would take one look at her and know something was terribly wrong. Still, Ava gathered herself up and made her way to the stairs bracing herself for the questions Jack would surely have.

She'd barely begun her descent down to the kitchen when the merriment from Jack's voice greeted her, "Good morning, Ava!" His smile was brighter than the sun was at this hour of the day. "I thought we could walk to school this morning. I hope that's okay."

She climbed down the rest of the staircase before turning to look at Jack. Immediately his disposition changed as he took in her tired appearance from a night of crying.

He rushed over to her, words quickly tumbling out of his mouth, "What's the matter, Ava?"

She watched as her mother registered the concern in Jack's tone and actions, her expression soon matching his. "Are you okay, Ava?" her mother asked as she also hurried over to wrap Ava in a hug.

"I'm fine," Ava lied. "I just couldn't sleep last night."

Her mother gave her a quick squeeze and then went back to finishing the dishes from her morning's baking. Jack, however, didn't move. He knew more than her mother did. She knew she'd have to tell the truth on their walk to school. She took a deep breath and then walked away from Jack, breaking from his stare that made her feel uneasy.

"You shouldn't have lied to your mom," Jack gently scolded her as they walked side by side down the sloshy, winter streets.

"I can't tell her what we've discovered yet, Jack. I don't know what she might do." Ava's mind was scrambled. She hated lying to her mother, but she needed to know more before she told her. Her mother would have questions that she wouldn't be ready to answer.

"Does she know about your painting?" Jack's question made Ava wince and he saw the answer in her reaction. "You must tell her, Ava. She's your mother."

Ava didn't feel like being lectured by her best friend, so she threw the question back at him. "Does your mother know about your writing?"

Jack was silent.

"I thought so." Ava crossed her arms as they walked, allowing the gloom of the day to settle over her. The houses and stores along the street were beginning to wake. Children slowly began pouring out of the doors on their way to school.

"I don't know what we should do, but Ms. Beckett was right when she said the truth is a huge responsibility." Jack let out a sigh and she could feel his shoulders sink, burdened by what they now knew.

Ava stopped walking. Jack turned to her when he noticed her sudden halt.

"Jack, I don't know if my gift is really that special. That painting in the book was an exact copy of mine, or should I say my painting was an exact copy of it. Is my gift really that special if it's already been done before?" Ava let a small tear race down her sullen cheek. She wasn't sure how she had any tears left to give.

"Oh, Ava." Jack's voice was smooth and warm, a calming blanket attempting to cover Ava. "I am so sorry. I thought you were distressed from discovering the real history."

He dropped his books and wrapped his arms around her in the middle of the streets of Dryden, allowing her to bury her face in the roughness of his hand-me-down coat that smelled of freshly sanded wood and spices from his mother's cooking.

"It's not that our gifts haven't been used before. Sometimes they may even look or sound the same, but that doesn't mean they aren't needed right now. Whoever painted that was needed then, many years ago. You are needed right now. Your gift is still special, Ava. You are still special." Ava melted into Jack's words, her heart grabbing onto the hope in them.

When Ava untucked herself from Jack's embrace and wiped her eyes with her coat sleeve to clear them, their surroundings came into focus. Several people stood frozen on the sidewalks scowling at both Jack and her.

"This town is so frustrating sometimes," Ava muttered under her breath, but Jack didn't share in her irritation. Instead, he smiled and waved at everyone looking at them which made some of the scowls turn to shock.

As he smiled, he talked to Ava through his teeth, "And if we don't change it, who will?"

He then took her hand to walk her the rest of the way to school. In that moment, Jack's actions made Ava think of her father. She imagined the people of Dryden had given him similar looks, and it made Ava smile. She let her smile grow and soon she was waving at the people of Dryden with Jack. Both making a scene that appalled anyone who saw them.

By the time they reached the schoolhouse steps, they were laughing. They were met by Mrs. Polly, and she did not match their smiles.

"You two are late." Her voice was firm, and her lips were as straight as a sharp, metal ruler. "Inside, now!"

Mrs. Polly stomped back into the schoolhouse leaving Jack and Ava on the steps outside.

"Don't let her annoyance take root in you, Ava. We get to prune what we grow in our heart." Then he dipped down in a graceful bow, playfulness dancing across his face. "After you, Miss."

A bubbly laugh escaped Ava's lips and her hand quickly covered her mouth, hoping Mrs. Polly didn't hear it. She gave Jack a small curtsey and then hurried inside to her seat.

The day droned on with more repeated lessons. Ava had caught herself slouching many times, succumbing to sleep. Her troubled night was wearing on her, and the worksheets felt tedious which lulled her brain into a heavy tiredness. Ava needed rest. She'd tell Jack they'd have to continue digging through the history of Dryden another day.

Finally, Mrs. Polly dismissed them for the day. Ava was sure she'd just sat through her longest school day ever.

"That was excruciating," she mumbled to Jack as they made their way down the steps outside of the schoolhouse. "I don't think I can go back to the bookstore today."

"I figured as much. You would most likely fall asleep during what could be one of our most exciting discoveries ever," Jack said as he offered her a small, sympathetic smile.

She was nervous Jack might want to go without her, but she should have known Jack would be more understanding. They parted ways and Ava made her way home slowly. Her feet felt like bricks trudging through the slush of melted snow and dirt.

She noticed spiraling smoke from their small chimney. Her mother was rarely home before her. As she opened the door, she smelled the warm aroma of cinnamon and the soft sound of her mother's whistling drifting through the air.

"Hi, Ava." Her mother had just closed the oven door and turned to greet her. "I thought cinnamon rolls might lift your spirits after your difficult night of sleep."

Tears began to tumble down Ava's cheeks, the guilt of keeping things from her mother finally breaking free.

Her mother hurried over to her, wiping the tears with her worn apron and asked, "What's wrong?"

Her mother gathered her up in a tight hug and Ava felt as if she was a soaked towel being wrung of all its water. Her mother held her until Ava's eyes were finally dry.

Ava looked up and said, "I have some things to tell you, mother."

"It's a good thing I made cinnamon rolls. Serious conversations require serious treats." Her mother kissed her cheek and let her go.

The cinnamon rolls sat between them, butter melting over their warmth. Her mother had poured her a glass of milk. Ava was nervous about telling her mother everything, but she now knew keeping things from her wasn't the answer. She didn't want to create problems between them. Her mother was one of the most special people she had in her life.

"I don't know where to begin," Ava said in a small voice.

"You can begin wherever it feels easiest. I'm not here to judge you, Ava. I just want to help you. It seems you've been carrying some heavy things by yourself. Let me carry them with you." Love poured from her mother's mouth through the words Ava's heart desperately needed.

Ava took a deep breath. "You know the paints you gave me?"

Her mother nodded.

"I'm really good at painting, but it's not just that I'm good. I don't even have to try very hard. The painting just happens, the brush creating whatever my mind imagines." Ava glanced up at her mother, unsure what her mother's reaction would be.

"I had wondered," her mother murmured through a slight smile. There was a softness in her eyes as if she understood more than what Ava had just told her.

"You aren't surprised?" Ava asked.

"No. I've watched your light begin to fade ever since your father died. I was worried it would completely go out. I've tried to keep it ignited, but I've also been struggling without your father. He was the one who brought all the fun and laughter to our home. I knew I couldn't replace that, but I was also scared of trying. Your father was much stronger than I am, and I feared what others would think. But since I gave you the paints, your light had begun to glow again."

Her mother still wore a smile, not allowing the sadness that usually came with mentioning her father to defeat her in that moment. Ava realized her mother was being strong for her and it gave Ava the courage she needed to continue.

"I want to show you how I paint, but first I need to tell you something else." Ava took a deep breath and sat up straight in her chair.

"I've read an old history book of Dryden. Not the ones we have now, but the real ones."

Her mother's smile fell. "What do you mean the real ones?"

"The history books that were taken away before they were replaced with new ones," Ava said confidently.

"There are different history books?" her mother questioned.

"I've seen them, mother. They are old, but beautiful. They talk about the creation of Dryden. I've just started reading through them, but there are several. All I know right now, is that the history we've been taught isn't the real history and that Dryden hasn't always been Dryden." Ava became quiet as she said her last words.

"What do you mean?" her mother asked.

"In the beginning, Dryden was called First Springs."

Her mother sat unmoving, processing what Ava had just told her. Ava hadn't known if her mother would listen or if she would immediately tell Ava she was wrong. She wasn't sure what was going on in her mother's head and heart, but Ava's were silent as she held her breath.

Finally, Ava's mother let out a whisper of words, "Your father was right."

16

I t turns out curiosity ran in the family. Ava's father had questioned the history of Dryden as well but had never been able to discover the truth. Ava still didn't know much, but it was enough that it lit a fire in her mother, too. She watched as her mother grew with excitement, which only made Ava's enthusiasm grow to show her mother the process of her painting.

She grabbed her mother's hand pulling her up the stairs to her room. She hurried—removing her supplies from their hidden place as quickly as possible. She spread them out on her desk and pulled out her small chair. She motioned for her mother to join her, and they both squeezed together, sharing the narrow width of the chair seat.

The paper and paints were laid in front of them.

"If you could go anywhere, where would you go?" Ava asked her mother.

She watched as her mother took the time to really think about it. Time passed as she watched her mother's cheeks become flushed with happiness.

"Have you ever painted a field of sunflowers?" her mother asked.

Ava shook her head, "I've thought about it, but I haven't."

"Your father used to tell me about these big, yellow sunflowers that seemed brighter than the sun. He told me he imagined them sprouting to the clouds, so tall you'd get lost in them like a forest. I'd love to journey through a sunflower field like that."

Ava picked up her paintbrush, choosing yellow to begin. She wanted to paint the most wonderful place for her mother to see. She hadn't yet told her mother about traveling through the paintings. However, her mother's reaction to everything else made her believe she'd choose faith when Ava revealed that secret.

She glanced over at her mother. She sat there with her eyes wide, anxious to watch her daughter begin.

"Ready, mother?" Ava took a deep breath. Painting with an audience made her a little nervous, even if it was her own mother.

"I'm very ready." Her mother smiled at her tenderly and then leaned over to place a kiss upon Ava's cheek. She must have felt Ava's nervousness because she added, "Just paint like I'm not even here."

Ava took the paintbrush soaked in yellow and began to paint.

She soon heard the murmur of chirping birds and felt heat bloom upon her skin, warmed by a sun that didn't exist in her room. Her head was filled with sunshine and happiness. The yellows felt energetic, and a smile spread across her face. It wasn't too long before she set her paintbrush to the side, the magic that existed within it now alive on the paper.

Ava soaked in what she had just created. She'd never seen anything like the field of bright yellows that laid before her. The sunflowers reached the top of the paper, a soft blue barely peeking behind their petals.

"This is the most beautiful thing I've ever seen." The words slowly fell from her mother's mouth.

Ava looked over at her mother, her eyes wide in amazement. Her mother's cheeks were flushed, and Ava didn't know why she'd never noticed it before, but her mother's lips were a beautiful, natural pink. She looked more alive with color than she'd ever seen her.

"It's pretty shocking," Ava stated.

"It might be shocking, but it's amazing, Ava. What you just did is one of the most incredible things I've ever seen." Her mother looked at Ava with tears in her green eyes. "The painting isn't just amazing. You are amazing."

Ava's eyes matched her mothers, both in color and in tears.

"There's more," Ava said, taking a great breath to give strength to her lungs to tell her mother the part about traveling through the paintings.

Her mother looked at her, waiting.

"I don't know how else to say this, except just to say it." Another deep breath and then Ava quickly said the next words, "I can travel through my paintings."

Several moments passed before her mother finally said, "What do you mean? Do you dream of these places after you've painted them?"

Ava shook her head, pulling a piece of her golden hair back into place behind her ear. She closed her eyes and then opened them again, "I go through the paintings. I don't know exactly how it works, but I close my eyes and believe myself there. Then when I open my eyes, I'm inside the painting."

She watched her mother sort through her thoughts. Ava began to wonder if the confession was too much for her mother to understand but then her mother grabbed her hand.

"Can we try?" Her voice was hopeful, and Ava knew she was trying to comprehend what Ava was telling her.

Ava squeezed her mother's hand and said, "I'd love to take you through this painting."

"So, we just close our eyes?" her mother asked.

"We hold hands, close our eyes, and believe ourselves to be in the painting. But mother, there's something else about the paintings I need to tell you before we begin."

Ava's mother looked at her and she could feel the trust that had woven itself between them.

"There is always the same man there. He knows me and I feel as if I've always known him. I just wanted to warn you before we got there, and you begin to worry."

Ava's mother smiled and Ava thought she had never looked so beautiful. She could tell her mother was willing to believe, too.

"I won't be worried. I'm ready," her mother said.

They closed their eyes with their hands wrapped tightly together.

When they opened their eyes, the sunflowers were so much taller than them that Ava laughed. Their surroundings glowed which made the yellow of it all, overwhelming. She felt as if they were being bathed in sunshine. She turned to her mother, and she wore a dress of the deepest blue. It was silk and it contrasted perfectly with the field of sunflowers that surrounded them. Her brown hair was glistening, and Ava realized that her mother wasn't plain and ordinary at all.

"Mother, you are beautiful," Ava declared.

Her mother blushed at the flattery and Ava wondered how long it had been since someone had told her that she was lovely.

At that moment, there was a man's voice, "Hello, Rose."

It was the first time Ava had heard her mother's first name spoken in years. The voice didn't belong to the man that usually greeted her in the paintings, but it was so familiar that tears sprung from Ava's eyes before she saw the man that matched the voice.

There he was, just as Ava remembered. Her father.

If time existed in the paintings, it stopped. Ava was afraid to breathe, afraid that any movement would somehow erase her father from being there. She didn't know what to say, but she wasn't the one to break the silence.

"Dillon." Her mother's voice was breathless.

Ava watched as her father ran to her mother, lifting her off the ground. They spun in circles, meshed in laughter and tears. Her father's golden hair matched her own. He was tall and strong, just as Ava remembered him. It had been so long since she'd last seen him and at that time, he had been frail and fading away. He set her mother down and then turned to face Ava.

"My beautiful little girl." The words tumbled softly out her father's mouth. "Look at how much you've grown."

Ava continued to stare at him. It was difficult for her to believe her father was there. Her father slowly took steps towards Ava, cautious in his approach.

"I..." Ava's words trailed off.

"It's okay, Avisha, it's me. It's your father."

"How?" she finally managed to ask.

Her father closed the distance between them and then knelt before her, his deep, brown eyes looking into her green ones.

"My body may have failed me, but I've never been lost. I've been waiting for you and your mother in this beautiful place." He smiled up at Ava.

Ava crumpled to the ground meeting her father there. A river of tears rushed out from within her. "I've missed you so much."

Her father gathered up her limp body and gave her the hug she had wished for every night as she fell asleep. It had been many years since her father last held her and the comfort soaked into Ava. Her mother joined them on the soft ground, and they were all together again, holding onto each other with a fierce joy.

Ava didn't want to let go, but she knew they couldn't remain there piled on the ground of a painting forever. So, she wiggled free and stared at her parents together once again.

"Oh, Ava, what a gift you've given me," her mother said. She had never seen her mother more glorious than in the glow of this painting. She could see gratitude and hope radiating from her.

"Ava?" Her father questioned. Her father had always called her Avisha. Her mother had begun to call her Ava after her father had passed.

"I call her Ava," her mother began. "I was afraid that it would set her apart at school since it is such a different name. I didn't want her to get hurt."

Her father nodded his head in understanding. Ava thought back to all her father must have gone through choosing to be different in a place that wanted him to be less than. Her mother must have been scared for Ava, the daughter of the man who represented everything the town of Dryden despised. She didn't blame her mother. She had tried to protect her.

Ava slowly stood to her feet and her father did the same. He gave a deep bow in Ava's direction reminding Ava of all the times they had pretended she was royalty in their humble home.

"Princess Avisha, what brings you to this beautiful field of sunflowers today?" Her father's voice boomed, echoing through the glowing sky.

Ava giggled, dipping into a small curtsey to return his bow, and said in her most proper tone, "I journeyed through a painting hoping to discover the most glorious place in all the lands."

"What is your discovery?" her father asked.

Ava shuffled her feet, turning her body slowly to take in their surroundings. It was at this moment she realized the flow of the silky dress around her legs, a beautiful green encompassing her. She started turning more rapidly, watching the richness of her skirt twirling magically around her until she became dizzy with excitement.

She let out a laugh from the rush of spinning and said, "I'm not sure I could have painted anything more wonderful than this."

Her father broke character, his face changing to something that was both soft and lively at the same time.

"You painted this place?"

Ava nodded, a blush creeping up her cheeks.

"Who gave you the paints?" he asked.

"Mother did." Ava smiled at her mother still seated on the soft ground beneath them.

Her father smiled down at her mother and then said, "It seems you have a gift in painting, Avisha. I always had hoped you would find what made you feel special."

Ava looked intently at her father, "What is your gift, father?"

Ava had been wondering what other gifts were out there, but she thought about her father's gift most of all.

Her father smiled with confidence and said, "I can turn anything to joy. It's not that you can't do the same, but for me it comes easily. No matter how hard something was, or how much something or someone may have hurt me, I could always find joy in my circumstances."

Ava thought about this and remembered how Ms. Beckett had told her if it feels like it is part of who you are, it's a gift. However, her father's answer puzzled her because it wasn't a skill like painting or writing.

Her father must have seen her puzzlement because he then said, "Gifts aren't always tangible, Avisha. Sometimes a gift is something that is seen in a different way."

Her mother finally lifted herself off the ground and joined them.

"Your father always said that I had a gift of helpfulness," her mother said slowly. "I wasn't sure how that could be a gift. Then one day, our neighbor fell down her front steps and broke her hip."

"Mrs. Edmund?!" Ava exclaimed.

"Yes, Mrs. Edmund. She was very bitter about the ordeal. Every meal we had, I made extra, and took it over. I'd help clean up anything when I delivered the food. For the first week, she scowled at me the entire time. By the time she was healed up enough, her scowl was gone, and she even managed to mutter a small 'thank you'. For me, it was easy to help her. It didn't feel like extra work and even the lack of gratitude never bothered me. It was at that moment, I knew your father was right. Most others would have been finished with the attempt of helping her on that first day or would have grumbled the entire time, but for me it was natural. I never lost my heart in it. In fact, it made me feel more alive in helping her."

Ava caught her father smiling fondly at her mother.

"You glowed during that time. It was one of the most beautiful things to see you embracing who you are," her father said. Then he looked at Ava and added, "Gifts are as unique as people are, but when someone discovers theirs and embraces it, you'll be able to see it. It's pure light."

Ava smiled at the thought of everyone in Dryden becoming light—a town full of people embracing who they were created to become and being allowed to do so was a magical thought.

"I hope one day I get to see the people of Dryden come to life," she muttered.

Her father walked over to her and embraced her once more. Ava melted into him.

"I don't think the time is too far away, Avisha." Her father looked down at her smiling and said, "It seems to me that there is a special girl that might inspire light once more."

Ava smiled back at her father, but nervousness filled her body as she pondered his words. She wasn't sure how she would be able to bring light back to the town when her father, who had been so full of joy, was not able to. She buried her head into her father's chest, clinging to the hope he had in her.

She felt her mother wrap her arms around her, too.

"I believe she can," her mother said, adding to the hope Ava felt.

"One more thing, Avisha," her father said, "When you discover a book about names, look yours up. I think you will find something incredibly special about who you are."

Ava promised, and then as suddenly as her mother and her were in the picture, they were back in the narrow chair holding onto one another.

17

Over breakfast the next morning Ava's mother laughed as she said, "That wasn't the man you expected to be in the painting, was it?"

"No, it wasn't." Ava returned the laugh.

Breakfast felt like a feast even though it was the usual toast and eggs. Ava had a feeling that the night before had just changed everything for her and her mother. There was a happiness in their home that hadn't been there the day before.

"Do you think we'll see him again?" Ava asked her mother.

She watched her mother contemplate the question until a soft, beautiful smile sketched itself upon her face. She glowed as wonderfully as the paintings.

"I know we'll see him again," her mother said confidently.

Ava nodded, taking a bite of her breakfast. She felt the truth in her mother's words. She knew they'd see her father again one day. He had said he was waiting for them.

"Well, what do we do now?" Ava's mother asked.

"What do you mean?" Ava replied, her mouth full of raspberry jam and buttered toast.

"We can't keep that kind of hope from others. It's exactly what this town needs!" her mother exclaimed.

"But what about your rule to keep my painting secret?" Ava asked.

Her mother's expression remained soft as she said, "I was trying to protect you, Ava. However, I think in protecting you, I may have kept you from what your heart needed most." She cleared her throat and stood up tall, "The rules no longer apply."

The rules no longer apply? her brain questioned while her heart jumped.

Ava didn't know how to respond. With no rules, there was no protection, and Ava realized that is what she feared the most. If she decided to share her gift, she was opening herself up to the possibility of hurt and rejection.

"How do I even share my gift?" Ava timidly asked her mother.

Her mother smiled at her, "I'm sure you'll figure that out."

Ava finished her breakfast, grabbed her schoolbooks, and headed for the door. She still had an entire day of school ahead of her, and she wasn't sure she would be able to keep her head in her studies after where she had been the night before.

"I'll be home late tonight," her mother said as Ava shimmied on her winter coat.

"I'll start supper. Thank you for breakfast, mother," Ava replied. She was about to head out the door when her mother's hands grabbed her and pulled her in for a tight hug.

"I love you so, Ava. Have a wonderful day." Then her mother placed a kiss upon the top of her head.

Ava began her trek to school realizing the streets of Dryden were continuing to grow with color. Today she saw the greens of spring beginning to make their appearance from the ground to the tops of the trees. The color was faint, but it was there.

"Hopeful, isn't it?" A voice caught her attention.

Ava turned and Ms. Beckett stood next to her, smiling.

"What is hopeful?" Ava asked, smiling at this woman she now considered a friend.

"The beginning of something that can become beautiful," she replied.

Ava noticed Ms. Beckett was staring at the trees and quietly asked, "Can you see the color, too?"

An energy danced in Ms. Beckett's eyes as she said, "I'm so glad for a world that has color. Something within me believes there is about to be a lot more of it soon." She took Ava's hand and squeezed it.

"Ms. Beckett, what makes you believe there will be more of it soon?" Ava asked, curious about the spark that remained in Ms. Beckett's eyes.

Ms. Beckett took both of Ava's hands, positioning themselves so they were facing one another squarely, and then she said, "I think if we don't hope for the good, we may never see it. A lot of people believe that seeing is what makes us believe, but I think it is in believing that makes us see."

The words made Ava's head and heart buzz with excitement.

"Well then, I believe you are right. I think there is going to be a lot more color soon," Ava replied before hugging Ms. Beckett.

Ava felt possibility growing within her, but she still wasn't sure how to share her gift. She did, however, know someone who would know. She needed to consult the man in the painting.

"It was wonderful seeing you, Ms. Beckett!" Ava beamed. "I must be off to school, but I will see you soon."

The school day passed quickly, and Ava was thankful for it. She missed multiple math problems, distracted by her desire to get home to paint. She was anxious to see what the man in the painting would tell her this time. She had told Jack over lunch that she wouldn't be able to go to the bookstore after school once again, but of course, Jack understood. He was also anxious to see what the man would tell Ava.

"I'll come by your house tomorrow," Ava told Jack as they parted ways after school.

"Promise?" he asked.

Ava sent him a small smile and answered, "Of course."

Ava practically ran home, her mind filled with visions of what she could paint. She burst through her front door and stumbled up the stairs, eagerness propelling her forward faster than her feet could carry her. She hurried to her supplies, grabbing them all in one huge scoop, and dumped them on her desk.

You can do this, her brain said, and Ava realized her head that was once full of criticism had turned to encouragement.

The painting in front of Ava looked different this time, as if it held a little more magic. It displayed a deep, blue ocean that spread as far as the eye could see. The night sky felt like a globe encircling the waters, its surface reflecting the glimmer of stars. It should have felt like the darkest scene she'd ever painted, but it felt like the brightest. She could feel the coolness of a breeze wrapping around her, goose-bumps sprinkled on the surface of her skin.

She closed her eyes and when she opened them, the beauty of the painting wasn't enough to prepare her for the place she found herself in. She looked up at the sky, glittered with the light of a million stars. The largest smile erupted across her face.

"Beautiful, isn't it?" His voice was beside her.

She turned to look at him. This man had become someone she didn't just expect to be there, but a man in which she found so much comfort in his presence. It was at this moment she realized they were in the middle of the ocean, standing in a small, simple boat made of wood. Their feet were bare. She was clothed in a simple, white dress but its softness made it feel like luxury.

"It's incredible. How many stars do you think are up there?" she asked, turning her attention back to the sky.

"Two million, six hundred thousand, and two," he replied.

Ava didn't question him. She felt he really could know the number of the stars.

"How wonderful it would be to exist as one of those stars. Their brightness is so magnificent," Ava whispered, wanting to believe in the deepest part of her heart that she could feel so radiant.

"That one." The man pointed to a single star hanging in the velvet sky.

"What about that one?" Ava asked.

"That one is you."

Ava laughed, unsure what he meant.

"That star is you, magnificent in brightness on its own. But do you think the sky would feel as bright if that star was up there by itself?" the man questioned her gently, his eyes warm and mesmerizing.

"No," she said in a small voice, shaking her head.

"The brightness of all the stars makes the darkness fade. It is light that brings hope to those who are looking for it." The man carefully turned in the boat to face Ava. "Avisha, there is light within you longing to be free like a star in the sky."

Ava closed her eyes and imagined herself sharing her gift freely, no fear in how it would be received. For a moment, she felt peace. Then she allowed her worries to surface.

Ava looked up at the man and asked, "But what if I'm all alone in the dark sky?"

The man smiled, "I know you won't be alone. There are people waiting for someone to be brave enough to encourage them to shine brightly, too."

Ava looked down at her bare feet, "But why me?"

The man's warm hands lifted her face to meet his eyes, "Why not you? You know you were made for more."

Ava's heart pounded furiously in her chest, the man's words proving that its constant desire for more was a truth within her that wanted to be heard. She felt strength pulse through her veins, a confidence like she'd never felt before. And it was at that moment she felt courageous in what she needed to do.

"I need to share my gift," she told the man with a tone of conviction.

He smiled at her before he gathered her up in the warmest hug she had ever felt. It was as if he was made of the softest blanket, his arms capable of a comfort she'd never known to want for. She melted into him. Any fear she had fell to the bottom of the boat.

"You do not need to be afraid, Avisha. You were made for a wonderful purpose. You have a beautiful gift that deserves to be seen by more than just the floorboards under your bed." The man winked at her.

Ava laughed and then she remembered how she felt as she had painted the place she was surrounded by, and her face fell slightly.

"What's wrong?" he asked her.

She took a deep breath, "When I painted this place it felt different. Will I always be able to travel through my paintings?" Ava asked.

"Avisha, your paintings are so much more than color and paper. The hope that exists within you lives in your paintings. That's what makes them special."

"What about you?" Ava asked. "Will you always be here?"

Ava had never seen such affection in the eyes of someone than she did in the man at that moment. She began to cry, and he gently wiped her tears.

"Avisha, I am with you always. My existence doesn't depend on a painting. I'm alive in here." He placed a finger upon her heart. "There's no need to cry. There never has to be a good-bye."

The truth in his words washed over her as if she'd been washed in the most refreshing rain. She jumped up into his arms and the boat wobbled beneath them. They both laughed as he held her.

"I'll never forget these times I've spent in the paintings," Ava said.

The man gently set her back down in the boat.

"It takes someone very special to create such beautiful things. I want you to remember that, Avisha. There will be those that believe what you share isn't special, but you must hold onto the truth."

"Sharing my gift is going to be hard," Ava admitted.

"But you don't have to do it alone, Avisha. I'm with you always."

The man then began to step out of the boat and Ava gasped.

"What are you doing?!" she exclaimed.

The man smiled and continued to step outside the boat. To Ava's surprise he was standing on the surface of the water. She was waiting for the sea to pull him under, but he remained untouched.

"Would you like to join me?" he asked her.

Ava was hesitant but then she reflected on everything that had happened to her since traveling through the paintings. There was so much that had been unclear to her before and so much that seemed impossible. However, everything had changed since she met this man. She had changed because of him.

She returned the man's smile.

"Do you trust me?" the man said as he reached out his hand to Ava.

Ava did trust him. She trusted him more than she'd ever trusted anyone. She would trust him with her life. She put her small hand in his and followed him out onto the water.

18

Ava knew what she needed to do. She stood up from her chair with so much energy that the wobbly legs scraped backwards against the rough wood of her floor. She marched over to her mirror, determination fueling her steps. The reflection had become a testament to Ava's belief that there was something more within her. She had once seen a dull version of herself, but now she saw her vibrancy. Her cheeks were blushed, her golden hair shimmered, and the green in her eyes glowed.

There was nothing ordinary about her. Something was alive within her.

She smiled at her reflection, joy dripping from the reflective surface.

"Dear friend in the mirror, it seems you may have been right. There is more than what is seen if we choose to look a little deeper."

She gave one more look at herself and then hurried out her bedroom door. She took the steps down to the kitchen two at a time, anxious for her mother to arrive home for supper. She would need help to put her plan in place and she knew her mother would be thrilled to help her.

Ava dug a few ingredients out of the pantry and began to make a simple stew for their supper. The room was soon filled with a savory aroma that made her stomach gurgle. She began humming a happy melody and it magically mixed with the spices in the air. She became so lost in the moment she missed the sound of the front door opening.

When Ava spun around to set the table for supper, her mother was there watching her.

Ava shrieked.

Her mother laughed and said, "I'm so sorry. I didn't mean to scare you. You are buzzing with such radiant energy, I just wanted to enjoy the moment without disrupting you."

She dashed around the table to wrap Ava in a warm embrace. Ava leaned in and giggled.

"I just didn't hear you come in," Ava finally replied after her heart had stopped racing.

"It smells wonderful, and it sounded wonderful, too," her mother muttered into the top of Ava's head as she placed a kiss amidst her silky curls.

Ava broke from her mother's embrace, "Let me grab a bowl for you. I have so much to tell you, and I'm going to need your help."

Her anxiousness took over again, moving her limbs more quickly than they were skilled at. She knocked a few things over in the process of finding a ladle to scoop some hearty stew for her mother. She rushed around, placing bowls of stew on knitted placemats.

She hurried to her chair.

"Please sit, mother," she said rather rapidly.

Her mother laughed, "You are filled with much momentum this evening."

Ava bit her lip, waiting for her mother to take her seat. She knew the plan she was about to describe to her mother would be one where her momentum would be greatly needed.

"Okay, what's this plan you need help with?" her mother asked with a smile as she lifted her spoon to take a bite of the stew.

The words tumbled quickly out of Ava's mouth, "I need to share my gift and I think the best way to do that is to paint as many pictures as I possibly can. I want the entire town of Dryden to be covered in color. I want the streets lined with images of beautiful places that most have never even hoped to believe in. I want everyone to see that there is something more than what they've been told."

Her mother sat silent, but not for long. "This is exactly what your father would do. It's such a grand gesture of faith to share your gift so openly. What do you need me to do, and when do we start?"

Ava's excitement grew with her mother's eagerness to help with such a grand plan. Nothing like this had been done in Dryden and Ava knew she would need the encouragement from those she loved most to follow through with it. It would be hard to worry about the possible consequences if she could hold onto the love and support of those who knew her best.

"I want to start tonight, but first I need to talk to Jack. I need him, too," Ava said.

"You best be off then as it is getting late," her mother said as she stood from her seat. She walked over to the front door, grabbing Ava's coat and hat.

Ava smiled as her mother helped bundle her to keep warm in the lingering winter cold. The sun had sunk below the earth and darkness had fallen on the streets of Dryden. With no streetlamps, Ava would have to rely on any light that happened to pour out the windows from the houses of Dryden.

"I'll be back soon," Ava said as she kissed her mother's cheek.

Ava walked slowly at first, light was as scarce as warmth in the air. Her toes in her boots began to feel the chill, and then Ava looked up.

Up in the blackness of the sky was one bright star. Ava immediately felt the chill fall away believing the bright star had been placed by itself on purpose. As she stared at it, she saw the faint glow of a second star make its appearance.

Hope began to hum loudly through her veins, and she quickened her steps to Jack's house.

Ava stood at his front door and before she could knock, the door was flung open and there stood Jack all smiles and smudges of dirt.

"Ava!" he exclaimed.

"What is all over you?" Ava asked.

Jack laughed as he said, "I was put to work after school today cleaning the entire wood shop."

If anyone else would have been put to work cleaning such a space, they wouldn't have been half as happy as Jack was about it.

"I need to talk to you," Ava said.

She peeked in behind Jack and saw his family at the kitchen table, grabbing food from different plates using no manners in their quest to fill their stomachs with the food Jack's mother had prepared. Her own stomach dropped a little at the possibility of sharing a meal with Jack's brothers.

"We can sneak on up to my room," Jack said, watching Ava as relief washed over her face.

Once upstairs, Ava shrugged off her coat, and began to tell Jack her plan of hanging hundreds of paintings all along the streets of Dryden. When she had finished, she was sure Jack's face would split from how large his smile had grown. It was practically covering half his face.

"I'm in," Jack said enthusiastically.

"I haven't even asked for your help yet," Ava said.

"But you were going to, right?" he asked.

"Well, yes, but..." Ava began.

"I'm in for all of it. You just tell me what you need from me." Jack pulled Ava into a sudden hug. "This may be the most amazing thing that has ever happened to Dryden."

Ava gently pushed away from Jack, "I just want it to be the beginning of the most amazing thing that has ever happened to Dryden."

Jack smiled and repeated, "The beginning."

"I must get home to paint. Before we can put the plan in place, we need all the paintings I can manage to create." Ava reached out and squeezed Jack's shoulder. "Thank you, Jack."

Ava snuck back down the stairs and scurried quickly out the front door, avoiding interaction with Jack's brothers.

As she began her walk back home, she looked back up into the sky and noticed a third star glowing beside the other two.

19

Ava painted with a determination she'd never possessed before. Days passed and her mother had to make a special errand to locate more paper for her as she was rapidly running out of materials. She hoped she had enough color in her palette to complete the task.

The plan was grand, and Ava felt the exhaustion of it from her brain cells to her fingers that became weary from holding the paintbrush for many hours each day. She also had begun to worry about how the town would react. She was about to reveal what made her special to a town that wanted her to remain silent.

"Can I do anything else for you, Ava?" her mother asked.

"I will need your help in the morning when I am ready to put the plan in place," Ava said. "Mother, I also am so grateful for the encouragement you've given me over the last few days."

"It's been as easy as breathing, Ava. I'll always be here for you no matter what," her mother replied as she smiled down at her, gently squeezing Ava's shoulders while Ava continued to concentrate on the painting in front of her.

The plan was simple in theory. She just needed as many paintings as possible to fill the streets of Dryden with their color and vibrant hope. She almost had enough. The painting in front of her would be the last one. It was a simple scene of a clearing in a forest. A cozy, red cabin was nestled in a thicket of soft bushes. It felt like it was tucked away, waiting for someone.

"This is the last one." Ava let out a relieved sigh. Painting may be her gift, but it didn't mean she wouldn't become fatigued from the work that came with it.

"It's beautiful," her mother said over her shoulder. "What happens next?"

"Tomorrow morning, early before anyone in town awakens, we fill the streets with paintings." Ava smiled at the thought of it. She imagined everyone pouring out into the streets, beginning their ordinary days. Her paintings would be there to greet them, hopefully jolting something within their hearts that also wanted to believe there was something more.

"Simple enough," her mother said. "I must go to work for a few hours. With spring around the corner, many have brought in several pieces to mend for the new season. I am so proud of you, Ava. You best get some rest before the early morning arrives."

Ava sat unmoved from her chair, unable to find the strength to stand after hundreds of paintings had held her captive to her desk. Her mother leaned down and hugged her while she sat. Ava took in a deep breath and with it the smell of her mother. She smelled of laundry soap and fresh air.

"I love you, mother," Ava whispered into her mother's thick hair that fell loosely around her shoulders, free of the bun she had once always worn.

"I love you so, Ava," her mother whispered back.

She heard the stairs creak under her mother's footsteps, and then finally heard the door open and shut. Ava stared at the stack of paintings that lined a wall in her room. An immense amount of color peeked out from them. It made Ava wonder how her palette had been able to create them all.

Suddenly, she heard a knock downstairs from the front door. She groaned as she slowly lifted herself out of the narrow, wooden chair. She made her way carefully down the stairs as blood began to flow back into her legs. She felt drained, but in a way that made her smile at the reason for her fatigue.

She finally made it to the door and flung it open.

Jack stood there holding a bright, red box with the most elaborate, golden bow glistening with sparkle and shine. Ava grabbed his arm and quickly pulled him inside.

"What is that?!" she exclaimed.

"It's called a present, Ava." Jack laughed.

"Did anyone see you?" Ava asked, her words coated with worry.

Jack set the present down to the side and grabbed Ava's shoulders gently.

"Breathe, Ava. Remember, we can stop worrying about the judgments of others." He released her. "Besides, I wanted you to have something special."

Ava's heart was racing. It wasn't the colorful box Jack carried that was causing her anxiety to rise. She was about to display over a hundred paintings through the streets of Dryden. It was a very big act of faith and hope.

Jack must have seen the distress pulsing through her because he quickly wrapped her up in a hug. She pressed her head into his shoulder and found herself holding onto him tightly.

"Ava," he whispered into her golden curls. "Everything is going to be more than okay. I know you are made for something more and I cannot wait for everyone to see that, too."

Ava pulled away from Jack looking up into his brown eyes.

"It isn't just about me, Jack. I want people to see what I see and to feel what I feel. I want the people of Dryden to see color again. I want them to dance in the streets like my father did. I want them to recognize that they were also made for something more."

Jack brushed a strand of her hair to the side and said, "All you can do is what you know you must do. You aren't responsible for everything else."

Ava's heart had begun to calm, and then she remembered the present. She peeked down at it resting on the floor. She'd never seen a present wrapped so beautifully.

"Where did you find the wrapping?" Ava asked.

"I may have had a little help from Ms. Beckett," he replied. "Do you want to open it?"

"Of course, I want to open it!" Ava squealed with delight.

Jack picked the present off the floor and walked over to the kitchen table. He set it down gently and Ava saw him take a deep breath.

"I really hope you like it," he sighed with anticipation.

Ava walked slowly over to the present taking in all its colorful glory. She hadn't opened something so full of vibrancy since she had unpacked her paints from the plain, brown sack weeks before. This time her head and heart were in sync and excitement flowed throughout her entire body.

She ran her hands down the side of the smooth box wrapped in red.

"It's almost too pretty to unwrap," she whispered.

She looked up at Jack. He was smiling at her, watching her every movement.

She gently tugged on the golden bow and watched it release its grip around the box. The ribbon fell to the sides, and she swept them away. She slowly tore into the paper, laughing at the feel of it. She couldn't remember the last time she'd received a gift with wrapping paper. Soon it was a bare, brown box. She lifted the lid and there was not enough air in her lungs to prepare her for the gasp that came from the shock of what she saw.

Inside, laid carefully among soft tissue, was a dress, but it wasn't just any dress. It was a bright, yellow dress. The sleeves were puffed, and lace was wrapped delicately around the bodice. Golden buttons shaped as sunflowers adorned the front. She slowly took one finger and ran it down the softness of the fabric.

"Do you like it?" Jack's question interrupted her surprise of the elaborate gift.

"How did you...? Where did you...?" Ava was speechless.

Jack laughed, "I knew it was the perfect gift! I wanted you to have something special to wear tomorrow. You deserve something as beautiful as your heart, Ava. I wanted you to feel bright and vibrant, wearing something like you wear in your paintings."

Ava wasn't sure how Jack had acquired such a beautiful dress. She also didn't know if he knew exactly how perfect the dress was. He didn't know about her conversation with the man in the paintings about the brightness of the stars, and although he knew she had seen her father, he had no idea it was in a field of sunflowers.

Ava fell to the floor and Jack quickly fell to his knees to meet her there.

"What's wrong?" The words rolled frantically off Jack's lips.

"Do you really think I can do this?" Ava was beginning to feel the significance of what she was about to do. "I don't know what is going to happen tomorrow."

Jack pulled her back into a hug while they sat on the floor and said, "Ava, I believe in you, but more than that, we do not have to fear the unknown. The unknown can also hold wonderful things. We've seen that. What if what you do tomorrow changes everything for the better? What if what you share is exactly what is needed?"

Ava leaned into Jack, taking hope and confidence from his words and his embrace. She knew he was right. What she had seen and how she had changed was something she couldn't keep to herself.

"Promise me something, Jack," Ava said.

"What do you want me to promise?" he asked.

"Promise me one day you'll share your writing, too. You always know exactly what to say. Someone else needs to hear your words."

Jack looked down at Ava, "I promise."

Ava took a deep breath, leaning into Jack's assurance.

Tomorrow was going to be a big day.

20

It was finished. They'd hung up every single painting. It was exhilarating work. Ava's lungs had never felt so full, brimming with excitement to tell everyone about what was possible. It was still dark, but Ava thought she could see sparks of light radiating from the paintings.

"Nervous?" Jack nudged Ava as he stood at her side.

Ava smiled and asked, "Would you be nervous?"

Jack laughed as he wrapped his arm around her shoulder. "Yes, I would be. I would also be enormously excited. I mean, look at all you've done, Ava. I've never seen you more joyful."

Jack was right. Ava felt purpose with every beat of her heart, and it was pounding so quickly that it created an upbeat rhythm of hope within her. She looked down at the beautiful dress Jack had gifted her, smoothing the radiance of it with her small hands.

"Part of that joy has to do with you," Ava said as she looked up at Jack. "This dress is perfect."

"The dress is only a reflection of the light I see within you," Jack said. "I better let you take your place. I'm so glad I am part of this, but this is your gift, Ava. I'm so excited to watch you shine today."

Ava flung her arms around Jack's neck, embracing him one last time before the world of Dryden would see Ava for who she was. "Thank you," she whispered into his ear before she broke the embrace.

Jack smiled before he left her at the steps of the white building that had always sat empty at the end of the streets of Dryden, as if the streets had all once meant to meet there.

"This is it," her mother began as she grabbed Ava's hand. "I'm so proud to be your mother."

Ava looked up at her mother and saw a tear slide down her soft cheek. She reached up and wiped it to the side with her thumb and said, "I was made for this."

Her mother looked down at her with loving eyes as she said, "Not everyone will be ready for this, Ava, but some will be. I'll be here no matter what happens."

She pulled Ava into a hug.

"I'm ready, mother," Ava said confidently.

"It takes someone very brave to do what you are doing today," her mother replied.

"It's not just about me anymore. As you have said before, we can't keep this kind of hope from others who desperately need it. It's time to be like my father." Ava smiled up at her mother. "I hope my paintings are as wonderful as his dancing in the streets."

At that moment, Ava knew she was ready for Dryden to see her gift. She knew there would be some who would reject her for it, but she wasn't concerned with those who weren't ready for what she had to share. She was excited to see what would happen to those who had also silently hidden their belief that there was something more.

Her mother left her side, leaving Ava alone on the steps. This next part was something Ava wanted to do alone.

A gentle sunrise woke up the houses in Dryden. The beams beautifully framed Ava's paintings, making the streets become the most charming art gallery. Ava sat on the concrete steps dripping with anticipation at what was about to happen.

As the sun's yellow became richer and more golden, the color from the paintings erupted along the streets. Ava gasped at the splendor of it all. Dryden may not have glowed with the same glory from her travels within the paintings, but what she now saw was one of the most beautiful things she had ever seen.

She took a deep breath when she saw a door along the street open, followed by several more. The people of Dryden were beginning their day but were soon frozen in place as if they had suddenly become concrete statues. The streets began to echo with breathless surprise.

Ava sat still, waiting for the stunned silence to produce something with noise.

Suddenly, Ava heard a child squeal with delight. She hurried to find the source of it and saw a young boy standing beside his mother pointing at one of her paintings. Even from a distance, Ava could see the spark of wonder in his eyes. Ava smiled and was filled with a quiet confidence from his response. His joy was a reminder that this was about more than herself.

Then it began. Ava heard the first cry of disgust.

"This is absolutely frivolous!" a man exclaimed.

The first criticism was joined by many more. The air soon swirled with hatred for what surrounded the people of Dryden. People were calling her paintings unnecessary, ugly, and even despicable. Ava watched as the little boy who had found delight in them, hid himself within the skirts of his mother.

This isn't about you, her brain offered the reminder.

Then a booming voice sounded, "Who is responsible for this display?"

Ava didn't hesitate. She had been waiting for this very moment. She stood up boldly and there was nothing timid about her steps as she made her way down to the streets below her. She stepped out among the people, her golden curls gleaming and her yellow dress matching the brilliance of the beams that fell over her.

"These are mine," she spoke confidently, calmness woven into the tone of her words.

A man walked up to her, and it was exactly who she had expected. It was the mayor. At one time Ava had been filled with fear anytime she had seen the man, but now she just saw the deep sadness in his eyes that were framed by thick, furrowed eyebrows.

"What are you wearing?" he asked with words that sounded like daggers.

"A dress," Ava simply replied.

"None of this belongs here. The paintings or the dress. Why would you want to corrupt the people in this town?" His words were bitter, and Ava felt the hurt in them, but she knew it wasn't what she had done that hurt him. She knew his reaction was one that came from years of suffering.

The next words she spoke caused a hush within the streets, "I don't think I'm the one who has corrupted this town. This town has long been corrupted, but it doesn't have to be. Hope is available to everyone, but we've been made to believe there is nothing more for us than what happens to us."

She felt his anger flare and then recognition came across his face, "You are the street sweeper's daughter, aren't you? The one who died?"

The words were meant to hurt and silence her, but she didn't let them. Instead, she found confidence within them as they reminded her of who she was.

She smiled brightly at the mayor and took a step toward him, "Yes, I am. You know what was so wonderful about my father? So many people in this town were cruel to him, but it didn't keep him from joy. The insults didn't steal his smile. The broken streets didn't steal his dancing. Even when he was lying in his bed, unable to move, my father still had hope. If you think you can take mine, you are wrong. Who I am isn't determined by what you say or think of me."

The mayor fumbled for words, his face turning red with anger from the truth she had spoken.

"Rules! The rules! You've broken the rules!" he finally managed to exclaim.

"With all due respect, Mr. Mayor, there are no rules. There have only been expectations and I'm aware that I am failing those," Ava replied calmly.

"You are just a girl. You don't understand," the mayor said scruffily.

"You were once just a boy. Did you not once wonder? Did you not secretly feel that there was something more for you? When I was younger and my father was alive, my heart vibrated daily with joy. I could see the magic in every small thing. The older I became, the more I was stripped of my wonder. However, my heart never gave up. It would still beat, hoping I would believe again. There is so much more to this life than what we've been told to see. I think if you take a better look at one of my paintings, you might remember what it was like to wonder."

"I don't need to see it more closely to understand that this isn't acceptable," the mayor was gruff in response, but his voice had lowered from a yell.

"What if I told you that one of these paintings was made especially for you?" Ava asked.

The mayor's expression changed slightly, a bit of curiosity peeking through his hostile demeanor that was slowly melting away.

He must say yes. Her brain and heart hoped together.

Ava broke her gaze from the mayor and slowly walked a few steps over to where she had intentionally hung the painting. It was the last one she painted; the little, red cabin nestled within the cozy trees. She had felt it was made specifically for him. She grabbed the painting and took it back to the mayor.

The mayor was still standing silent, confused about what he should do.

Ava gently placed the painting in his hands watching as he struggled with his thoughts. His hands slowly began to move apart to rip the painting in half.

There was a collective gasp in the street.

The little boy who had found wonder in the paintings courageously ran up to the mayor, hands outstretched, and said, "No! Please! I want to know what you see."

Ava could feel the hope in the boy's words, and she added, "I promise if you open your heart up and really look into the painting, you'll see something more."

Ava hoped she was right, but something within her believed something would happen if he could choose to hope.

The mayor's voice became quiet as he looked up at Ava with embarrassment and whispered, "I don't know how."

"Let me show you," Ava replied gently. She stood by the mayor, arms pressed together. She could tell he was barely breathing. "First, take a deep breath through your nose and close your eyes."

To her surprise, he did just that.

"Now open them and really look at the painting. Take it in with open eyes and an open heart. I'll do it, too."

Ava looked deeply at the painting. She took in the peace that it exhibited until she felt the gentle breeze of pine-fragranced air. She felt the tickle of grass as it fluttered around her legs. She opened her eyes and saw a bird in the most exquisite color of orange land on a branch above the little, red cabin.

Surprise filled Ava when she felt the mayor standing next to her.

"What is this place?" he asked. His voice was quiet, but Ava could feel a breath of excitement in it.

Her heart thumped at the realization that he had believed enough to travel through the painting. If the mayor had enough hope, that meant the people of Dryden may soon begin to hope, too. Ava felt tears rushing down her face. She hurried to wipe them away.

She looked over at the mayor and discovered she wasn't the only one crying. The mayor's anger had completely fallen away.

"I think you may know where we are," she said.

Suddenly they both were interrupted by the opening of the cabin's door. There in the threshold stood a woman, her red hair matching the cabin, flowing beautifully down her shoulders.

The mayor gasped.

"Lucy?" he whispered.

"Do you know her?" Ava asked gently.

"How?" the mayor asked, but Ava could feel the answer in his question, too. He knew where they were.

Instead of answering his question, Ava said, "It's amazing how those we lose are never lost to us forever. Hope is a beautiful thing, isn't it? We can claim to know a lot of things, Mr. Mayor, but there is so much more to life than what is understood or seen."

"Can I go see her?" His voice was still quiet.

"Of course. I'll wait for you here," Ava replied.

The mayor took off toward the little, red cabin where the woman he called Lucy waited for him. She smiled through her tears. Her heart felt warm realizing that her gift could become more for others. Her gift had the possibility to connect others with something so much bigger than herself.

"Incredible, isn't it?" The man had once again appeared beside her.

She smiled up at him and said, "I have a question. Do we truly travel through the paintings?"

The man laughed, "What do you think?"

Without missing a beat, Ava replied, "I think my paintings show others that there is something more."

Today had confirmed that she was given a gift to share hope with others. She would never forget this day when the change in her had begun the change in someone else.

21

There was a sparkle dancing in Ava's eyes as she walked down the streets of Dryden. They had been completely transformed over the last several weeks. Color was bursting from every brick, every door, and every flower that had been planted in pots lining the sidewalks. Music trickled out the windows of every home and shop, filling the town with joyful tunes.

She stopped to watch children playing inside their home, smiles lighting up their living room. On a wall, she spotted one of her paintings. It was in a silver frame hanging in the middle of a wall, but it wasn't alone. Drawings the children had made covered the wall around her painting. Ava blinked back tears.

When Ava had chosen to share her gift, it had inspired so many others to share theirs. Beauty and hope were alive and flowing not just in the streets of Dryden, but within the homes. It also wasn't just things you could see physically. People's gifts of hospitality, joy, helpfulness, and more had turned scowling neighbors to ones that embraced one another with warmth and happiness.

She had never been alone, but it had taken courage to inspire others to link arms and change the town for the better.

She watched as the mother of the children entered the living room and started tickling them, all of them eventually collapsing to the floor in a fit of laughter. The mother's eyes were glistening. Ava couldn't remember the last time she'd seen so much joy in a home in Dryden.

She smiled to herself and then continued her walk towards Jack's house. The freshness of spring was beginning to make itself known. Trees were turning bright green and grass was daring to poke up from the barren ground. Ava was filled with so much anticipation to see a colorful Dryden in spring.

"Hello, Ava!" A man smiled at her, mixing concrete in a large wheelbarrow preparing to repair the streets of Dryden. Another man was installing streetlamps. The town was about to shine brightly even in the darkness of night. Ava beamed at the thought of the streets being restored and becoming exactly as her father had once hoped. He would have been so excited to dance in what would become the streets of Dryden.

"Hello!" she replied with a smile and a wave. She made a silent vow to herself to dance in the streets for her father when they were completed.

As she turned the corner towards Jack's home, tucked behind the woodshop, she heard laughter. Jack's brothers were outside tossing a ball between each other. Ava had never seen Jack's brothers playing and the sight warmed her heart.

"Catch!" One of the brothers threw the ball in Ava's direction. She opened her arms, a thrill of a giggle escaping her lips as she caught the ball and wrapped it up close to her chest.

"Is Jack home?" Ava asked as she walked towards them, releasing the ball, and gently tossing it to the brother closest to her.

"He's inside writing," the brother replied.

"Thanks!" she replied and skipped off to the front door of Jack's home.

She opened the door, and the smell of spices greeted her as they always did. Ava was sure that Jack's mother had a gift of cooking. She turned to shut the door and as she did, color caught her eye above the mantle of their fireplace. There, was the painting of the beach where Jack and she had traveled together. It was encompassed in the most elegant, wooden frame. She quickly made her way towards it. She reached out to softly trace the wooden frame with her finger.

"Beautiful, isn't it?" The voice of Jack's mother greeted her. "Almost as beautiful as the heart of the girl that painted it."

Ava turned around with a small smile of gratitude and said, "Whoever made the frame made something beautiful, too."

"That would be Jack's brother, Tommy. It turns out he has a knack for crafting more delicate pieces with his skill of woodworking." Jack's mother smiled proudly at the frame around the painting. "You know, Ava, you've inspired so much good. I don't know if you understand exactly what you have done. Dryden has completely changed because of you. My family has completely changed because of you."

Ava blushed at the flattery, but she knew it wasn't just her that had inspired such changes.

"You are too kind, but I can't take the credit for the transformation Dryden has experienced. I think we all know there is something more that has caused hearts to change." Ava smiled at Jack's mother. "Can I go see Jack?"

"Of course, you can go see Jack. He's up in his room lost in another story he is writing." His mother continued to smile, joy radiating from her sons embracing their gifts.

Ava flew up the stairs, reaching Jack's room at the end of the hallway quickly. His door was slightly cracked, and she took the chance to peek inside. He was hunched over his desk, his pen moving with a furious, calculated rush. He'd stop just long enough to grab enough ink to take him a few words further, not wanting to stop longer than he needed to.

It was a rush to watch someone else embracing their ability. She felt the energy that was buzzing within his room, powered by Jack stepping into his potential. She didn't want to interrupt, but she had also promised Ms. Beckett she'd help at the bookstore that afternoon.

She gently knocked on the door.

Jack looked up, startled. Then a huge smile burst from him.

"Hey, Ava. Let me just finish this thought." He looked back down at his paper and after a few more dips in the ink, he put his pen down. He stretched out, his chair rocking on its back two legs.

"What are you writing about?" Ava asked Jack.

"It's not a story ready to be shared yet, but I think it is something you will love. It's a story about a boy lost in the ocean. He becomes shipwrecked on a distant island. He feels as if his life doesn't matter, but he discovers something amazing that makes him begin to believe differently."

"Believe differently? Perhaps that there is something more?" Ava winked at him. "It sounds incredible, Jack. I cannot wait until I can read it."

Then, Ava laughed.

"What are you laughing about?" Jack asked, curiosity washing over his face filled with color.

"I just never imagined I'd come to your house and be greeted with so much happiness. Your brothers are outside playing, your mother is downstairs beaming with pride while cooking something that smells divine, and you are up here writing stories that weeks ago we wouldn't have been allowed to read in school. Life has changed so quickly."

"It is pretty incredible, isn't it?" Jack shared in her laughter. "Dryden doesn't seem so dry and barren anymore."

"No, I have a feeling it feels like it once had before the color began to drain from it," Ava mused.

A few weeks after Ava had displayed her paintings for all of Dryden to see, they had ventured back to the secret basement of the bookstore. They'd dug the old history books back out and picked up the final volume. First Springs had been renamed because it had lost its sense of refreshment, no longer a place where people thrived but a place where people only survived. The people of First Springs had allowed loss to define them. Whether it had been loss of loved ones, loss of dreams, loss of status, or loss of possessions, the people had clung so desperately to their losses in the world that hope had evaporated from the hurting town.

People had become bitter, allowing their hurts to infect every aspect of their life. The color in First Springs had drained, unable to be seen by those who no longer believed in something more. People faded as quickly as the color had.

"I need to go to the bookstore. I promised Ms. Beckett I would help her put more of the books from the basement on the shelves, but I wanted to give you this." Ava pulled a folded piece of paper from the pocket of her jacket.

She handed it over to Jack and he gently unfolded it.

It was a painting of Jack and Ava at the beach. Ava had painted it from memory. They were dressed in their swim clothes, hands held, standing at the edge of the ocean as it washed over their bare feet. In the sand next to Jack was another set of footprints.

Jack's voice cracked as he said, "I love this, Ava."

Ava bent down and gave Jack a hug. "Promise me that we'll always make sure one another remembers."

Jack hugged her back. "I'll never let you forget, Ava. And for what it's worth, I always told you that you'd look best if you traded your melancholy for a smile."

Ava laughed, "Well, you were right, but I best be going. See you tomorrow?"

"Tomorrow," Jack replied.

Ava left his room filled with gratitude that she had Jack. He reminded her so much of her father. She had needed his encouragement more than she ever knew.

She made her way back down the streets and went in the back door to the bookstore. She could have gone in through the front door, but it felt more special knowing this place was the doorway in which she and Jack had discovered something that helped change everything.

She made her way to the front and saw Ms. Beckett stocking the shelves.

"I'm here, Ms. Beckett!" Ava exclaimed as she gave her a surprise, hearty hug.

"Well, yes, you are!" Ms. Beckett laughed ecstatically, adding to her beautiful laugh lines.

"Have you found anything interesting today?" Ava asked as she released Ms. Beckett from the hug.

"I discover something interesting every day. These shelves have never been so full and colorful. It's a beautiful sight. It makes you enjoy owning a bookstore again." Ms. Beckett smiled brightly.

Ava grabbed a box and began placing books on the shelves, adding even more color and hope back to the bookstore. Suddenly, a bell rang.

"When did you install a bell?" Ava asked Ms. Beckett.

"The day you displayed your paintings," Ms. Beckett replied.

Ava smiled at the thought of it. The brightness of her star had inspired the brightness of Ms. Beckett's. The man had been right, but Ava had already known he would be.

She picked up a small turquoise book that had the most elaborate, foiled lettering. Her heart picked up its pace as she read the title.

Names and their Meanings

She fumbled the book open, her eyes quickly searching for the meaning of her own name. She had promised her father she'd look it up. She had hoped such a book existed. It had to be important if that was the only promise her father wanted her to make in that special moment.

Then it was there. Tears filled her eyes.

Avisha: Gift of God

Lost in her own thoughts, she'd already forgotten the bell meant someone had entered the shop.

"Hello?" A gentle voice interrupted her happy crying. "I need some help locating a book. What's your name?"

She looked up smiling at the man and said, "My name is Avisha."

ABOUT THE AUTHOR

First, thank you so much for reading this book. When I asked God to light the steps in front of my feet, He did so with Ava's story. Or should I say…Avisha's. This book was written for my children, but I am so excited to see it in the hands of others.

I'm a writer, a mother, and a wife. I always wanted to be an author, but my current career involves ghost writing. That's just a fun title that means I write content for other people without my name attached to it. My dream is to continue writing my own stories. Maybe one day I'll have shelves full of my own books!

We live on a humble homestead of three acres. We have a milk cow that we milk daily, pigs that love belly scratches, chickens that love to peck at the backdoor to say 'hello!', and incredibly fluffy cats that snuggle more than they mouse. Soon we will have a large garden including a garden grown only for beautiful flowers. Just like Ava, we really love to see our world come to life with color.

Before this gets too long, what I really want you to know about myself is that I haven't always listened to God. I, too, have experienced life drained of all color. Who I am today is not possible without choosing to believe who I am in Jesus Christ. There is hope alive in you if you choose it. There is a gift within you if you look for it. There is so much more to life than what the world wants us to believe.

This story was one I cried through because I could feel hope growing through the pages as Ava became awake to the truth. It can be your story, too. Jesus can change everything.

IN HOPE AND LOVE,

Shelbey Kendall

Special thanks to my mother who used so much of her extra time to help edit this book for her grandchildren. Putting a book together in a few months is not the easiest accomplishment but I was thankful I could count on someone I could trust with the story.

Love you momma!

The Boy Who Wanted to Be Found

CHAPTER ONE

The water was so cold Dante felt as if icicles clung to the fragments left of his torn clothing, weighing him down further into the ocean. He took a deep breath above the rippling surface and plunged forward once more. He was almost there. The shore that felt miles away was finally within his grasp. As he swam, one of his feet hit the sand below the frigid water. He scrambled to stand. When he did the water pooled around his waist.

As he emerged from the ocean to stand on the beach, he was struck with a new panic. He may have made it to the shore, but it was void of any signs of life. He frantically scanned his new surroundings. There were no people, no houses, and no boats anchored. He looked back over the vastness of the sea, the blackness of night beginning to mesh into the darkness of the water.

Dante shivered, the coolness of night beginning to sweep across the deserted beach, making the pebbles of warm sand turn frozen. He looked down at his hands and saw his usual tanned complexion changing into a lucid blue. He needed to find warmth, and fast.

His bare feet stumbled through the shapeshifting sand. He was in a race with the sinking sun, and he had an irrational fear that the wild waters would pull him back in if he allowed fatigue to keep him on the shore.

Dante's arms were empty, unable to grab anything from the boat's wreckage as he swam to the nearest shore. He wished for a soft blanket to wrap around his trembling body.

He continued forward, faltering as the sand sunk beneath him, his legs becoming stiff from the desperate swimming in the freezing water. His jaw began to quiver, and he felt a hot, salty tear scalding his frosty cheek as it fell.

If only he could cry enough to bathe in the warmth of his own misery. The thought of a bath made Dante feel as if the sandy beach were made of snow. His legs gave into their weakness, and he fell to the ground.

In his head he could hear his father chiding him, *you are going to catch your death boy!*

It was possible. The ending to the story of his life could very well conclude alone on an unknown beach. He was sure no one would come looking for him. It was a death that made sense for the life he lived. One where no one knew where the boy had gone or where to even find him if they bothered to look.

No one had cared to ask where he was going when he prepared his scrimpy boat with the meager possessions he had accumulated.

He had set sail six days before, pushing away from the dock without any well wishes from anyone.

In the defense of the citizens of Amias Shores, he hadn't told anyone.

It had just been him for the last three years. He lived in a small shack on the outskirts of town, barely surviving on the coins he managed to earn from running errands or scrubbing windows. Occasionally, he'd arrive home to find a tiny sack of supplies at his doorstep, sometimes a few logs to burn in the crumbling fireplace to keep him warm enough through a winter's night.

His parents had both died, leaving him behind to fend for himself.

His mother had died giving birth to him. He learned of her death when he was four years old. The knowledge of the way she perished caused Dante to carry a heavy burden. If he had never been born, his mother would still be alive.

His father had been a hollow, unfeeling man. He never said a kind word to Dante, or many words at all. Neighbors had told Dante his father was once the type of man everyone wanted as a friend. He was helpful and laughed at everyone's jokes, whether they were good or not. He smiled all the time and when he married Dante's mother, there wasn't a happier man alive. When she died, his heart died along with her.

Dante had learned how to be unseen and unheard. He never feared his father hitting him, but he hated the lack of affection. He had never known what it was like to be loved.

He began to close his eyes, welcoming in the bitter end. Suddenly, he caught sight of a yellow glow from within the dense forest of trees in the distance. The forest looked impossibly far away, but the glow beckoned him. Did he have enough within him to achieve two life-saving treks within the same day?

A burst of strength powered his frail, weary body to stand. He took a deep breath of night air, its chill biting at his lungs as he swallowed. He lifted one foot, watching it sink into the sand. Then he lifted the other foot, following the path of the first. Step after step, he slowly walked towards the forest.

He heard the crashing waves beginning to fade into the distance as he closed the gap between the ocean behind and the unknown of the woods ahead. He stopped to gather his breath that was beginning to fail. The air around him felt dense and each breath he took made his body feel heavier than the moment before.

Maybe he wasn't meant to make it to the forest.

Did he even want to?

Dante sank down to his knees, allowing his exhaustion to overtake the small amount of hope he still had within him. Would death be so bad? What exactly was he living for anyway?

He had always felt invisible, lost in the blur of the lives of others that felt more purposeful than his own. If he chose to succumb to the persistence death, maybe at least he'd become someone through the mystery of his disappearance.

Maybe they'd erect a tombstone over a grave void of his body that read...

Here Lies the empty grave of the Boy That Was Lost...

Dante Banks

At least in his death, his name would be known. If no one loved him alive, maybe they'd at least love the mystery of his disappearance.

The wind began to whip through the thick, salty air. Dante's unruly, black hair that needed a trim fell over his eyes. He took his hands clothed in cold sand and shoved his hair to the side.

Dante looked up at the starless night sky and in a whisper said, "If there is anybody out there listening, I'm tired of trying to figure out what the point is. I've been lost forever."

He paused and let the flood of all the tears he had left pour down his hopeless face. Even if he saved himself this night, would the next day be worth it? He wasn't so sure anymore.

In one last desperate attempt he closed his eyes before falling to the cold ground and said, "If I'm worth being found, can you please find me now?"

...to be continued.

www.ingramcontent.com/pod-product-compliance
Lightning Source LLC
Chambersburg PA
CBHW020600250626
47154CB00004B/1297